THE PHANTOM
of Five Chimneys

Betty Ren Wright

Chapter One

He wanted to terrify them, but he didn't know how. He had tried slipping inside the door in the evening and into the living room where they sat after dinner. He'd walked among them, brushing against arms and legs, but no one had noticed except the little girl—the blind one. She'd asked her mother if there was a window open!

Was that all he could be now—a chilly breath of wind? Raging, he'd returned to the beach. Now he stomped along the ribbon of wet sand, leaving no footprints. There must be a way to show them he was there, watching, hating, still guarding his kingdom.

He stopped at a piece of driftwood. Narrow and gnarled, the wood was about the length of a tall man's arm. One jagged end looked like a cluster of fingers. He raised it with difficulty and held it in front of him.

An arm, he thought. It would do for an arm. And that

could be just the beginning! There was driftwood scattered up and down the beach, and fallen branches in the woods. If he was clever enough, he could send the intruders packing in no time.

He began to laugh. It was soundless laughter, but the sleepy gulls stood up and ruffled their feathers uneasily.

"It was supposed to be a *true* adventure, Daisy." Miss Mackey tapped a stubby finger on the paper in front of her. "I asked you to stay after class because I wanted to talk to you before I gave you a grade."

Tacky Mackey, that was what the girls at St. Elizabeth's called her. Hair flying in every direction. Safety pins holding her blouse together. Runs in her stockings. But nice, everyone agreed. One of the nicest.

"I really was alone all night." Daisy Gorman's face felt hot. "It happened the way I wrote it, Miss Mackey. My mom was away on an assignment, and the lady who stays with me was in a car accident on her way to our apartment. There really was a storm, and the power really went out." She paused.

"Fine, so far." Miss Mackey's finger tapped again. "Being alone in a storm was an adventure, I'm sure. But was there really a burglar? Did you really hit him with a flashlight and tie him up and call the police?"

Daisy stared out the window. She could see her classmates playing soccer in the field beyond the dormitory.

Tap, tap, tap. "I'm waiting, Daisy."

"Well, no, there wasn't a burglar," Daisy admitted, at last. "But there could have been. I did think I heard someone trying to break in. It was so scary!"

4

Miss Mackey sighed and picked up a red pencil. She put a big *D* at the top of Daisy's story. "I'm sorry to end the school year this way," she said, "but I have no choice. You're a good writer, but you let your imagination run away with you. You do that a lot, young lady."

She handed the story to Daisy, and then, unexpectedly, she smiled. "I have to admit it was fun to read," she said. "Have a pleasant summer."

Daisy folded the paper so she didn't have to look at the *D*. "I'm going out West with my mother," she said. "We're going down the Colorado River on a raft."

Miss Mackey's smile faded. "Well, have fun, whatever you do," she said coolly.

"You too." Daisy hurried out of the classroom and was halfway down the stairs before she realized what had just happened. Miss Mackey didn't believe she was going rafting on the Colorado River. She considered going back, but a glance at her watch told her it was too late. If she didn't get to the dorm in a hurry, she'd miss her mother's telephone call—the most important call of the whole semester. The reservations were made, everything was set, but there was always the chance that something would come up at the newspaper where her mother worked. *Just a very small chance*, Daisy told herself, and started to run.

The river trip was a celebration to mark the end of the school year and the end of her mother's biggest reporting assignment so far. The other girls were going to camp or to Disney World or to visit grandparents this summer— the usual stuff. This time Daisy Gorman was the person everyone else envied.

"Daisy! Wait for me!"

Daisy looked back and stopped, reluctantly. Marna Weber was cutting across the lawn in front of the dormitory, plowing, heavy-footed, through a bed of daffodils.

"We're losing," she reported when she caught up, as if the soccer game were the most important thing in the world. "Too bad you aren't playing. You're the best." She planted herself in the middle of the narrow walk and looked at Daisy expectantly.

"No, I'm not." Daisy tried to edge around Marna and failed. "Heather Graves is the best. Everybody knows that. Anyway, I'm in a hurry, Marna. Sorry."

The girl's thick features reddened. "That's okay," she said, but Daisy knew it wasn't. Some people could make you feel guilty over nothing at all, and Marna was one of them.

"My mom's calling from Chicago about something important at exactly four-thirty," Daisy explained hurriedly. "I don't want to miss her."

Marna's hurt expression vanished like magic. "Oh, sure," she said. "I'll see you later, okay?" She backed off the sidewalk and sat down, obviously without meaning to, on the bench at the entrance to the dorm.

The third-floor telephone was ringing as Daisy pushed open the front door. She raced through the lobby and up the stairs, disappointed that she hadn't been there for the first ring. She wanted to tell her mother how excited she was. *Ten whole days of doing stuff together,* she thought, *just like a real family.* As much like a real family as it could be, with only two people.

"Hi, sweetie. You sound breathless."

"I am. I ran up the stairs."

"Oh, to be young again!" her mother teased. "I can't remember the last time I ran upstairs." She paused. "I *am* doing a lot of running, though. Work and more work—"

"Is everything okay?"

"Well . . ." There was a silence. "I'm afraid—"

"Our trip is going to be so terrific!" Daisy said quickly. "I think about it all the time."

"Oh, Daisy!" Her mother took a deep breath. "Hon, I'm so sorry! We're going to have to put off the trip for a little while. Not a long time—a week or ten days, tops. Something's come up—a dream assignment I can't turn down. I'm going to cover a worldwide conference on AIDS."

Daisy sank, cross-legged, to the floor. Paper scrunched in her skirt pocket—the story with a *D* on it. "You promised nothing would happen this time," she said in a flat voice. "You absolutely promised."

"I know." Her mother sounded tired. "I certainly didn't *want* this to happen. But I'll be back soon."

"Back?" Daisy repeated. "Where are you going?"

"New York first, then London. But here's the *good* news, Daisy. You don't have to be stuck with a sitter this time. Something really nice happened last night."

Daisy pressed her forehead against the wall and didn't reply. She wanted to cry. She wanted to jump out the third-floor window and break her mother's heart.

"Shall I tell you what happened?"

"Okay."

"A Mrs. Graves called. She said you and her daughter are friends, and they'd like you to spend some time at their Lake Michigan beach house. It's a couple of hours north of Milwaukee. Apparently they inherited the house a few months ago and moved into it in January."

Daisy sat up straight. "Mrs. *Graves*?" she repeated. "Are you sure it was Mrs. Graves?"

"I make my living getting the details right, dear," her mother said dryly. "Believe me, it was Mrs. Graves."

"Why would Heather invite *me*?" Daisy wondered. "She could ask anyone. She has a zillion friends."

"But you're the one she wants," her mother said in an aren't-you-lucky voice. "It sounds like fun, much better than moping around the apartment here. And I'll know you're having a good time, so I won't feel so guilty about postponing our trip." She waited. "It's okay, isn't it? Shall I call Mrs. Graves and tell her you'll come?"

"I guess so." Daisy frowned at the telephone, pleased but puzzled.

"If you don't want to go, say so now, Daisy. Mrs. Carpenter has already promised she'll stay with you if you'd rather come home."

"I'd rather be with Heather," Daisy said. Mrs. Carpenter watched soap operas all day and made meat loaf every other night.

"I'll call Mrs. Graves right away," her mother promised, sounding relieved. They chatted a few minutes more and said good-bye. Daisy sat with the buzzing phone in her hand for a few seconds; then she stood up and wandered down the hall to her room, her head in a whirl.

Heather Graves was perfect—everyone at school agreed. Her family was perfect, too. Mr. and Mrs. Graves came to all the school programs and important games. Sometimes her older brother and her grandparents were there as well, laughing together and calling each other funny nicknames. Together, they formed a magic circle, with Heather in the middle.

Daisy wondered if they'd give her a nickname, too.

☻

The dining room at St. Elizabeth's was long and narrow, with twenty round tables. Crisp white tablecloths, pale blue napkins, and tall candles at the head table made the room inviting. After three years, Daisy still felt a thrill of pride and belonging each time she stepped through the swinging doors.

Tonight, though, she had other things to think about. She wanted to tell someone what had happened, but it had to be the right person. Her best friend, Jane Rosenberg, was having dinner with her aunt, so there would be an empty chair at table five.

Just inside the doors, Daisy stood on tiptoe, stretching until she could see table nineteen. Heather was already seated, her sleek dark head moving from side to side as people called to her. Was there time to push through the crowd right now and thank her for her invitation? Daisy was still hesitating when Dean Hartman rang the dinner bell at the head table. It was the signal for everyone to sit down.

For the next few minutes the girls were busy passing bowls of salad and stew and baskets of fresh rolls. Then Sara Cartman caught Daisy's eye.

"So, when are you leaving for Colorado?" she demanded. "Saturday or Sunday?"

"Neither," Daisy replied. Amazingly, the word didn't hurt. "My mom has to work. I'm going somewhere else."

"Where?"

Daisy concentrated on buttering a roll. Heather's invitation still seemed too much like a dream to talk about it. "Somewhere just as nice."

"Really?" Sara rolled her eyes. "Tell me."

Daisy shook her head. Sara would say, "Why did she ask *you*?" If she didn't say it, she'd think it, which would be almost as bad.

"Then don't tell," Sara said crossly. "Who cares?" She began whispering to the girl on her right.

Daisy ate fast. She listened to her classmates' chatter and nodded once in a while, but her mind was busy planning the evening. She decided she'd go to Heather's room after study hour to thank her. It would be easier without a crowd around.

When the bell rang again, signaling the end of dinner, Daisy was the first person on her feet. "See you later," she called over her shoulder as she hurried toward the entrance, only to find Marna Weber once more blocking her way.

"Did you get your telephone call?"

"Just," Daisy told her. She tried to keep walking, but Marna moved backward in front of her.

"What did you talk about?"

Daisy stared. Marna could be a pest sometimes, but she wasn't usually nosy.

"I mean"—Marna looked flustered— "did she tell you about our beach house? Are you coming?"

Suddenly the gruff voice seemed very loud, drowning

out all the noise in the crowded dining room.

"What do you mean?" Daisy's own voice was hoarse.

"You know what I mean. My mother telephoned your mother and your mother told you . . . but you don't want to come, do you? I can tell!"

"My mother said Mrs. *Graves* called her," Daisy explained painfully. "I thought—"

"My mother *is* Mrs. Graves." Marna's eyes narrowed as she realized why Daisy was confused. "You thought it was Heather's mom who called!" she wailed. "And you wanted to go, but now you know it was *my* mother and you don't want to!"

"I do want to," Daisy said, desperate to quiet her. Dimly, she remembered that Marna had been allowed to go home early the previous Christmas because her mother was being married.

"I don't believe that." Marna shoved her fists into the pockets of her skirt and stuck out her lower lip. "You're going to make up a story so you don't have to come. You'll pretend you're sick or something."

"I will not." Daisy blushed, since she'd been thinking about getting sick at that very moment. Flu, maybe. A weak heart. Leprosy! "I'm just surprised, that's all. I didn't know your mother's name is Graves."

"Well, it is," Marna said sullenly. "But it isn't mine, and it never will be. And now you've promised, so you have to come, even if you break your leg or get pneumonia. You can't get out of it."

Daisy felt like wailing herself. "I said I'd come, didn't I?" she snapped. "So quit talking about it. We'll have a good time."

But there was no pleasing Marna. "No, we won't," she said. "It'll be awful! You'll wish all the time that you were somewhere else, and my mother will pretend everything is great, and my stepfather is horrible. You'll see—it'll be awful!"

Daisy wanted to walk away, but she couldn't. Marna's misery was like a wall around the two of them, shutting out the other girls who edged by.

Of course it will be awful, Daisy thought. She wasn't going to Colorado. She was going to be Marna Weber's houseguest. And it was too late to jump out a window or get leprosy.

She was stuck.

Chapter Two

"My mother said we should wait outside the dorm," Marna said stiffly. She stood in the doorway of Daisy's room, an overstuffed suitcase in each hand. "She won't like it if we're not there."

"I'm ready," Daisy snapped. It was the first time they had spoken since their conversation in the dining room two nights earlier.

She picked up her suitcase and backpack and followed Marna down the stairs. *I hate this,* she thought, her eyes on Marna's hunched, unforgiving shoulders. Mrs. Carpenter and her soap operas would have been more fun.

They went outside, into weather as dreary as Daisy felt. A layer of thin clouds hid the June sun, and darker ones were piling up in the west. Daisy dropped her bags next to Marna's, close to the curb, and waited. She wondered if the other girls were laughing at her as they hurried by. Jane was the only person she'd told about the mixed-up invitation, but most of the girls knew that the raft trip had been postponed. They must be wondering why she was waiting with Marna now.

"This is it," Marna said suddenly. She stepped off the curb as a brown minivan pulled up in front of them. "You sit in front."

"Darlings! It's good to see you! Put the luggage in the back, Marna love." The pretty woman behind the wheel patted the seat next to her and gave Daisy's arm a squeeze as she climbed inside. "You're Daisy, and I'm Trish Graves, and that's Marna's little sister, Patty, in the back. We're so pleased that you're coming for a visit. I can't begin to tell you!"

"Thanks, Mrs. Graves." It was a cool reply, but it was all Daisy could manage.

"Trish," Marna's mother corrected her. "I've only been Mrs. Graves for six months—I'm not used to it yet."

Marna yawned noisily from the backseat, but her mother didn't seem to notice. She talked without a pause about the weather, about the girls' end-of-the-year tests, about the traffic that roared by on either side as they headed north. Daisy nodded and smiled and wondered if Marna had fallen asleep. She was startled when a small voice from the backseat broke through Trish's chatter.

"What color is your hair?"

Daisy turned to look at the little girl behind her. She had a sweet, thin face and a halo of fuzzy blonde curls like her mother's. Her eyes were huge and milky blue, and she seemed to be staring over Daisy's left shoulder.

14

Startled, Daisy realized Patty couldn't see. She felt a wave of anger at Marna for not bothering to mention it.

"My hair is brown," Daisy said. "It's not as pretty as yours, but it shines when I brush it. My mom thinks it's too long," she added, "but I like it."

Patty nodded, satisfied, and Trish Graves smiled at Daisy. "Patty has a thing about hair," she said. "I think she's going to be a hair stylist when she grows up."

"Am not," Patty said. "I'm going to be a swimming teacher."

Marna spoke for the first time since they'd left St. Elizabeth's. "You don't know how to swim," she said flatly.

"She can learn!" Trish exclaimed. "She *will* learn if she wants to. After all, she's only six. Don't be so negative, Marna."

At that moment a streak of lightning split the sky ahead of them, followed almost at once by rolling thunder. Sheets of rain flooded the windshield.

Trish groaned. "I was hoping it would wait till we got home," she murmured. "Every time it rains this hard, I'm reminded of that terrible night—"

"It's just rain," Marna cut in. "No big deal!"

Daisy leaned back and made up a story. *It looked like an ordinary storm, but it wasn't. Suddenly the wind lifted the car, and when it settled back on the road, it was heading south, toward Chicago. "Oh, dear, I guess we'd better just take you home, Daisy," Trish said sadly. "This visit was simply not meant to be."*

"Here's our turnoff, thank goodness!"

Daisy gasped as the car swung off the highway onto an almost invisible side road.

"We're just a half mile from the shore now, Daisy," Trish said, sounding relieved. "If the house doesn't look very inviting, you'll have to take my word that it's beautiful when the sun is shining."

"Like a castle," Patty said softly.

Marna said, "Yeah, right."

They rounded a final curve and turned into a rutted driveway that wound between tall pines. Firewood was stacked on one side of the road.

"That was my grandparents' root cellar." Trish pointed at a small stone building with a wood door. "Those thick walls kept their vegetables fresh all year. And there's the house. Welcome to Five Chimneys, Daisy!"

Across a scraggly lawn a long, gray-shingled house loomed in front of them. There were gables in the sloping roof and a row of tall, dark windows on the first floor.

"Gerald must be working in the basement," Trish said. "He's always busy."

"See all the chimneys?" Patty asked proudly.

Daisy counted them out loud. "You must have lots of fireplaces," she said.

Marna snickered. "Only two of them work," she remarked. "*If* someone remembers to bring in firewood."

"We'll have a fire tonight," Trish promised, ignoring her. "A fire is lovely on a stormy night, even in summer."

☠

The rain blew out over the lake while they were having their dinner. When the thunder faded, Trish opened long dining-room windows to the sound of gurgling rainpipes.

"Listen to that!" Gerald Graves joked. "Our own

private waterfall." He smiled at Trish and at Daisy, carefully avoiding Marna's glowering expression.

Daisy had already decided she liked Marna's stepfather. He was short, round, and almost completely bald, with a face that glowed with contentment as he looked around him. He was quite a bit older than Trish, Daisy thought, but they seemed just right together.

"Picture this room full of guests, Daisy," he said, gesturing grandly. "The walls will be painted and the chandelier will be working, and suddenly—BANG!" They all jumped as he leaped from his chair and staggered toward a window. "I've been shot, and it's up to *you* to find out who did it!" He pointed at Daisy, who stared at him in astonishment.

Trish giggled. "Gerald's telling you, in his own strange way, that next summer we hope to turn Five Chimneys into a bed-and-breakfast. Won't that be fun? It's something he dreamed about all the years he was working. Now he's retired, and as soon as he saw Five Chimneys he knew what we ought to do with it. We're going to have wonderful Mystery Weekends, with actors to stage a make-believe crime. Our guests will have to look for clues and decide who's guilty. Of course," she added breathlessly, "there's still a lot of work to do."

"Everything will get done," Gerald said, returning to his chair. This time he included Marna in his confident grin. "We're all going to help!"

Marna stared at her plate.

"I inherited this house from my father last fall," Trish explained. "He lived here with his older brother for many years, but when Uncle Morgan died, my dad moved away. I guess he wanted a taste of city life. He married in the East, and he never did come back to Five Chimneys. My mother said he couldn't bear it here, for some reason, but he wouldn't sell it, either. I hope he'd approve of it becoming an inn."

"Of course he would," Gerald boomed. "He'd love knowing other people were enjoying this beautiful place!"

Daisy looked around doubtfully. The dining-room wallpaper was streaked, and there were scars in the bare oak floors. Five Chimneys seemed a long way from being ready for paying guests.

"You're going to bring us good luck, Daisy," Trish said quickly, as if she'd guessed what Daisy was thinking. "I just know it! You wanted to come to Five Chimneys, and I'm sure many other people will want to come, too."

Daisy smiled uncomfortably, and Marna said, "Hah!"

"I'm going to make cookies for the people who stay with us," Patty announced. "And I'll show them where everything is."

"You bet you will," her mother said warmly. "And you'll do a good job of it, sweetie. When we've had our dessert, you can start by taking Daisy down to the beach."

☠

"Mystery Weekends!" Marna muttered. "That's such a dumb idea!" They were following Patty down the steep flight of stone steps that led from the lawn to the beach below. Marna had two fingers hooked firmly around the waistband of the little girl's shorts, but Patty pretended not to notice.

"We can go out to the end of the pier, Daisy," she called over her shoulder.

"Big deal," Marna grumbled. But Daisy noticed that she stayed close to her sister even after they reached the bottom of the steps. Together, the girls crossed the sand and walked out on the pier, with Patty in the middle.

The air after the storm was calm, and mist lay like a blanket just above the water. At the end of the pier there was a long bench.

"Sit down, Patty," Marna ordered. "You're not supposed to walk around out here."

Patty touched the bench. "It's wet!" she protested.

"Then you'll have to stand still," Marna said irritably. "You could step off the edge just like that!" She snapped her fingers.

Daisy shivered. The water made whispering sounds against the pilings, and the mist swirled around them. *Spooky,* she thought. *Any minute now the body of a drowned sailor will come floating by. He'll reach up and grab my ankle and—*

"I think your house would be a *great* place for a mystery weekend," she told Marna, to stop thinking about the sailor. "My mom's boss went to one in New England, and he loved it."

Marna rolled her eyes. "Gerald won't do it right. He doesn't know how to do anything. If my real father was here it might work, but Gerald will mess it up."

"Where is your real father?" Daisy asked. "Does he live nearby?"

"He's in California." Marna's gruff voice softened. "But someday he's coming back, and he and my mother will make up, and we'll all move to California together."

"With Gerald?" Patty asked. She winced when Marna laughed.

"Of course not with Gerald. He's not part of this family no matter what he thinks."

Patty stood quietly for a minute more. Then she took a cautious step back.

"I'm going in," she said. "It's scary out here."

"We'll go in a few minutes," Marna told her, but Patty jerked away and started along the pier, dangerously close to the edge. Both girls leaped to take her hands.

"Hurry!" Patty said, pulling them along.

"What's the matter with you, anyway?" Marna demanded. "Just because I think Gerald is a jerk—"

"No!" The little girl sounded close to tears. "Somebody's coming! Somebody's sneaking!"

Startled, Daisy and Marna looked up and down the beach. To the north the sand continued below the cliffs, ending at a breakwater barely visible through the mist. To the south, the cliffs were lower, and where they ended, trees crowded close to the water.

"There's no one coming," Marna scoffed. "Who would come along here?"

But Patty was not convinced. When they reached the foot of the stone steps, she broke away and scampered up them like a monkey, on all fours. Her panic was catching. Daisy found herself scrambling, too.

At the top of the steps, Marna grabbed her sister's hand again and led her across the lawn. "Hurry up," she called over her shoulder. "If she gets weepy, my mother will blame me."

Daisy hesitated on the top step. "I'm coming," she

called, but she couldn't resist looking back at the beach. Far down the strip of sand, she thought she saw something tall and narrow move jerkily through the mist. It vanished, then lurched into sight again.

I'm seeing things! she thought. She rubbed her hand across her eyes, and when she looked again the beach was empty. She started to run toward the house, with Miss Mackey's scolding voice echoing in her ears.

You let your imagination run away with you. You do that a lot, young lady.

Chapter Three

When she woke the next morning, her bedroom was flooded with sunlight. Daisy sat up and switched off the bedside lamp. The room, with its white-painted furniture and bright rag rugs, looked more cheerful than it had the night before. She dressed quickly, trying to forget that this was the day she and her mother were supposed to be on their way to Colorado.

From downstairs came the sounds of Patty's high-pitched voice and Gerald Graves's deep one. The smell of frying bacon filled the air.

"We're in the kitchen," Trish called as Daisy started down the creaky steps.

She made her way through the dining room and out to the big kitchen at the back of the house. The table was cluttered with cereal boxes, a milk carton, and a bowl of fruit. Gerald was busy at the stove.

"Sit next to me, Daisy," Patty shouted. "I'll tell you which cereal is best."

"Maybe Daisy would rather have bacon and eggs," Gerald said. "Just give your orders to the chef—that's me."

"Cereal and toast, please," Daisy said. "That's what I . . . uh, we, have at school."

"The orange juice is in the fridge," Marna muttered. She didn't look up, but at least, Daisy thought, she was talking. The night before, she had huddled in a corner reading until bedtime, while Daisy and Patty played a game called Detective. Using narrow, waxy sticks, they had taken turns shaping "clues"—a bird, a wagon, an arrow. Patty had shrieked with delight when Daisy, her eyes closed, had hesitated or guessed wrong. The little girl seemed to have forgotten her fear on the beach, but for Daisy, the memory of their frantic scramble back to the house had hovered like a black cloud over the evening. When she went up to bed, the tall windows in her room had seemed to dare her to look out.

Marna spoke again. "We can go swimming today if you want," she said, staring at the back of the cereal box as if the words she spoke were printed there.

Trish shook her head before Daisy could reply. "Oh, I don't think so, dear. The water will be like ice. It takes a long time for a lake this big to warm up."

"No, it doesn't," Patty protested. "We want to go swimming."

"Try wading first," Trish suggested with a smile, "before you put on your swimsuits. You may change your minds."

"I won't," Patty protested, and Marna shrugged. She seemed to welcome another reason to sulk.

"If you do go in the water, be very careful," Gerald Graves said, tilting his head in Patty's direction. "There's a wind, and the waves could be rough."

Marna looked at him sourly. "We're not babies," she snapped. As soon as breakfast was over she took Patty's hand and led the way out the back door.

In spite of the brisk wind, the air was warm, and heavy with a Christmas-like smell of pine. Daisy followed the sisters around the house and down the steps to the beach, where they slipped out of their sandals.

"Hurry up!" Patty dragged Marna toward the water, then squealed with surprise as the first wave licked her ankles. "It really is cold!"

Daisy took a couple of steps into the foam and retreated. The icy water made her feet ache.

"It's okay," Patty insisted, tugging Marna's hand. "Let's keep going."

Marna pulled back. "It's not okay. What's the fun of freezing to death?"

"But I want to go in," Patty begged. "I have to get used to it so I can learn to swim."

"Forget it!"

Abruptly, Patty sank down on the sand. "I could do it," she said softly. "It's not too cold."

Marna stared at her for a moment and then turned to Daisy. "Stay with her," she ordered. "I'm going back to the house to get something."

When they were alone Daisy settled, cross-legged, next to Patty and gave her a hug. "Don't feel bad," she said. "The water can't stay this cold very long. I think . . . I think somebody must have thrown a million ice cubes in the lake, and we just have to wait for them to melt."

Patty's mouth twitched. "You're making that up," she said.

"I didn't think you liked the lake so much," Daisy went on cautiously. "Last night—"

Patty moved away from her. "I like the lake," she said after a moment.

"But something scared you last night, didn't it?"

"I heard a funny noise." Patty's voice dropped to a whisper. "I thought I did, anyway. Like something scraping in the sand. Way off." She turned to Daisy hopefully. "Did you hear it, too?"

"No," Daisy admitted. "You have very good ears."

Patty nodded. "I hear lots of stuff Mom and Gerald don't. The noise was spooky."

Something scraping in the sand. The blanket of sunshine covering them didn't stop the goose bumps popping on Daisy's arms. She glanced quickly down the beach to where, the night before, she thought she'd seen something tall and thin move through the mist.

"I don't hear it now," Patty assured her, as if she'd been reading Daisy's mind. Both girls jumped when Marna spoke behind them.

"I brought the clothesline from the basement," she announced, managing to look bored and pleased with herself at the same time. "I'll tie it around your middle, Patty, and you can wade by yourself. I'll give it a tug if you go too far."

Joyfully, Patty scrambled to her feet and waited while

Marna fastened the rope around her. When the knot was firm, she walked fearlessly into the water.

"I wish I had a little sister," Daisy said wistfully. "Has she always been blind?"

"She was in a car accident three years ago," Marna said. "It wasn't anyone's fault," she added quickly. "I guess she's used to it now."

"Used to it?" Daisy repeated. "How could she get used to it?"

Marna didn't answer. The girls watched silently as Patty edged farther into the lake. The water reached her knees, and Marna gave the clothesline a gentle pull.

"When she gets tired of this we can go for a hike along the beach if you want to," she offered grudgingly. "We can look for stones."

Daisy looked at the lonely stretch of beach and the dark woods at the far end of it.

"I think I'd rather stay here," she said. "Maybe later." She was trying to say no as politely as possible, but it didn't work.

"You're bored to death already," Marna growled.

Chapter Four

Rain battering the windows woke Daisy the next morning. The tall trees edging the lawn were swaying in the wind, and whitecaps dotted the lake.

"Well, I know what I'm going to do today," Trish announced at breakfast. "I'm going to bake bread. I don't do it often, but homemade bread will be a nice touch when we start taking in guests, so I'd better practice. Patty, will you help knead?"

"Need what?" Patty looked puzzled until her mother explained. Then she was delighted with the idea of "punching" the dough.

"And I'm going to start painting the bookshelves," Gerald said. "I have one set for every bedroom now. What are you girls going to do?"

Marna scowled. "What *can* we do?"

"How about giving Daisy a tour of the house to start

with?" Trish suggested. "This storm can't last all day."

"Yes, it can," Marna retorted.

Daisy decided she'd never known anyone so determined to be miserable.

After breakfast she followed her classmate out to the front hall. "You've already seen the downstairs," Marna muttered. "Big deal. And the basement's full of spiders. If you want to see them, I'll wait up here. I can show you the other bedrooms, if you want. There's not much to see, except . . . oh, well, come on."

"You don't have to . . ." Daisy began, but Marna was starting up the stairs.

"There are eight bedrooms and only two bathrooms," she grumbled. "I suppose Patty and I will have to share a room when those dumb Mystery Weekends start. If anyone actually comes, that is."

She threw open one door after another as they walked down the long upstairs hall. All the bedrooms were furnished like Daisy's, with white-painted furniture and rag rugs. In the Graveses' bedroom, framed photographs covered one wall, and the bed in Patty's room was crowded with dolls and stuffed animals. Marna's room was bare; her suitcases lay open in one corner, and the top of the dresser held books in uneven piles.

"Nobody lived in the house after my grandfather moved out," Marna said. "It was a mess when we got here. Mom and Gerald have been buying secondhand stuff and fixing it up ever since." Her tone suggested this had been a waste of time.

"Why didn't your grandfather live here?" Daisy wondered.

28

"Because he hated it," Marna said matter-of-factly. "He grew up here, and I guess he liked it then, but by the time his older brother came back from the Second World War, their parents had died. My grandpa wanted to move away, but his brother wouldn't leave. They stayed here for a long time, but when the brother died—that was Great-uncle Morgan—my grandpa took off. He moved to Boston and got married and had my mother and never came back."

They had reached the end of the hall and faced a dark wooden panel, elaborately carved. Daisy had noticed it before, but now she realized that it was another door, much bigger and heavier-looking than the rest.

"This was Great-uncle Morgan's room," Marna said. "Uncle Morgan the weirdo. My mother says she doesn't know what to do with it, so she's just going to leave it for a while." She opened the door and motioned Daisy inside.

The room was larger than the other bedrooms. Heavy velvet draperies framed the windows, and the furniture was oversized and dark. High-backed armchairs stood on either side of a brick fireplace.

"Look at that painting over the mantel." Marna sounded as if she were enjoying this part of the tour. "That's Uncle Morgan. He hired an artist to paint it."

Lightning flashed across the windows as Daisy crossed the room. The man in the painting had a fierce and angry face. He wore a dark red robe and was seated in one of the high-backed chairs next to the fireplace.

Daisy didn't know what to say. "Why is he wearing a bathrobe?" she asked finally. "Was he sick?"

"That's not a bathrobe," Marna said scornfully. "He was a wizard. He wore that robe when he was casting spells."

"A wizard?" Daisy started to laugh, then stopped. Marna was serious.

"He really was a wizard. Look." Marna crossed to the mantel and took down a book. "This was his—*The Book of Spells*. You can tell it's old. And there are other books like it in the bookcase."

Daisy took the dusty book and opened it. The yellowing pages were printed in narrow columns. There were long lists of strange, unfamiliar names, and the type was so small and so old that she could hardly read it.

"This doesn't prove anything, Marna," Daisy said uncertainly. "Your uncle couldn't have been a wizard. They're not real. They're fun to read about, like Merlin in the King Arthur stories, but that's all."

"He was real," Marna insisted. She looked around the shadowy bedroom. "He probably cast his spells right here. Can't you tell from his picture that he was different?"

"Well, he was certainly no ray of sunshine!" Gerald Graves looked in at them from the doorway. "Morgan Trier was a cranky, unstable loner before the war, and a dangerously unbalanced man afterward—that's what Trish's father told her."

"That's not true!" Marna said angrily. "He was a real wizard. I don't care what *you* say." She seemed to have forgotten she'd called the man a "weirdo" just a few minutes earlier. "You shouldn't talk about our family that way."

Gerald's smooth face turned pink. "No need to argue," he said soothingly. "Actually, having a wizard in the family could be good for business when we start our Mystery Weekends. We'll probably have a waiting list for his room. Anyway," he continued, "I just came by to round up candles and oil lamps. The last time we had a wind like this we were without electricity for twelve hours."

He crossed to the fireplace and took an oil lamp from the mantel. "Don't look so worried, Daisy." He chuckled at her expression. "We have several of these lamps. Do you know how they work? You lift up the glass part—it's called the chimney—and light the wick sticking up from the bottom. You can adjust the flame with this knob on the side. Nothing to it."

"Do you think the power will go out again?" Daisy didn't like the thought of being alone in the dark in an unfamiliar room.

"Probably not." He gave her a reassuring pat on the shoulder and left, whistling as he walked down the hall.

As soon as he was gone, Marna snatched *The Book of Spells* from Daisy's hands. "I need this," she said grimly.

"What for?" Daisy was still thinking about the possibility that the power might be cut off.

"I'm going to make Gerald disappear," Marna declared, as if it were the most natural thing in the world. "He doesn't belong here. I'm going to make him disappear so that my dad can come back to live with us again."

Daisy stared at her. "You're joking," she said.

"I am not." Marna looked up at the portrait. "Uncle

Morgan was a wizard, and I'm his grandniece. So I can be one, too. I found the book when I was here for Easter break, but I didn't have time to study it then. Now I do. You can help me if you want to," she added.

"No, thanks." Daisy went out into the hall. There were a million things she would have liked to say to Marna, but she knew they wouldn't make any difference.

You're being silly.

You have a great family, and you don't even care.

I wish I'd never heard of Five Chimneys.

I wish—

"See you later," Marna said behind her, and slammed the door to Uncle Morgan's room.

Daisy went to her room, threw herself on the bed, and stared up at the ceiling. She thought about her mother and wished they could talk for just five minutes. What would her mom say if she knew about Marna and the weirdo wizard and the rain and the chance that the power might go out?

Hang on to your sense of humor, hon.

Daisy groaned. Life at Five Chimneys wasn't funny. *I should have pretended I had the flu when I had the chance,* she thought. Compared to Marna, Mrs. Carpenter and her meat loaf would have been great.

It didn't help when she rolled over and discovered that Gerald Graves had left the oil lamp from Uncle Morgan's room on the table beside her bed. A book of matches lay next to it. Squat and ugly, it somehow looked as menacing as the man in the portrait who had used it long ago.

Chapter Five

The rain stopped while they were eating dinner, but by the time the girls went up to bed that evening a new storm had swept over Five Chimneys.

Daisy snuggled under the bedclothes and listened to the drumming raindrops. This evening had been better than the last one, mostly because, surprisingly, Marna had been more cheerful. She'd even joined in the Detective game for a while, much to Patty's delight. It had been cozy, with the card table set close to the fire while Trish and Gerald watched a baseball game on television. The picture was fuzzy and sometimes disappeared for seconds at a time, but no one seemed to care. Gerald said Cubs fans were used to suffering.

The stabs of lightning came faster, making sleep impossible. Daisy slipped out of bed and went to the window. Trish's dainty bedsheet curtains weren't heavy enough to keep out the sight and sound of the storm, but they would help. She pulled a panel across the glass and then hesitated, staring into darkness.

The pale strip of beach appeared and vanished, as if she were seeing it in bursts of light from a flashbulb. She watched for a few moments, wondering at the force of the wind that sent waves scrambling across the sand. Then, as she was about to close the second panel, an especially bright streak of lightning lit up the whole beach. At its far end, close to where the cliffs ended and the woods met the water, something moved.

"No!" She said the word out loud, wanting to be mistaken. Her eyes were playing a trick on her, showing her something tall and narrow that walked on the beach in the middle of a thunderstorm. She waited, shivering, and when the lightning flashed again, the beach was empty.

Could it have been a tree branch broken off by the wind? She closed the second panel and hurried to the other window to cover that one, too. It wasn't a branch. It wasn't anything.

"What's wrong?"

The voice behind her was so unexpected that Daisy gave a little yelp of surprise. Marna stood in the doorway, wrapped in a fuzzy green bathrobe.

"I saw the light under your door," she said. "Are you scared of the dark?"

"I'm not *scared*," Daisy told her testily. "The wind was making so much noise, I couldn't sleep."

"Neither could I." Marna closed the door behind her. "I've been thinking about how you were sort of tricked into coming here. Now you're not having any fun, and it's my fault. You can go home if you want. I'll tell my mother you thought you were going to Heather's."

Daisy felt a rush of relief. She opened her mouth to say, "Go ahead, tell her." Then she pictured Trish's face and thought about how hurt she and Gerald and Patty would feel when they found out she wanted to leave.

Marna waited. Her feet were set far apart as if she were braced for a blow.

"Don't tell her," Daisy said after a brief pause. "I'm fine. Your mom is really nice to me, and so is your . . . so is Gerald."

"Uh-uh." Marna shook her head. She didn't want to hear anything good about Gerald.

"And Patty is great," Daisy went on. "You're lucky."

Marna narrowed her eyes. "Too bad my real dad isn't here," she said. "When he lived with us, everything was perfect." Her face softened, and for a moment she was almost pretty. "What's your dad like?"

"He died. A long time ago." Daisy didn't want to talk about her own family, or lack of one.

"Didn't your mother want to get married again?"

"I guess not," Daisy said. "She's too busy."

Marna nodded approvingly. "That's good. I bet you have fun—just the two of you."

Lightning struck close by with a resounding crash. The bed lamp flickered, and Daisy bit her lip. Marna when she was being friendly was as hard to talk to as when she was being mean. "My mom works too hard to have fun," she said, then yawned, hoping her visitor would take the hint.

"Oh." Marna's face reddened. She opened the door. "Well, if you change your mind about staying, it's okay," she said hastily, and padded out of the room.

As the door closed, lightning flashed again, followed at once by a burst of thunder. Daisy jumped back into bed and shut her eyes. The storm must be right over them now. She could see explosions of light through her eyelids, and thunder shook the bed. Maybe if she read for a while . . . She opened her eyes and discovered that the bedside lamp was no longer lit.

She sat up, too startled at first to remember that Gerald had put the oil lamp in her room. Then another lightning flash showed her the book of matches he'd left within easy reach. *Lift the chimney, light the wick* . . . his words came back as she reached for the matches.

The first two refused to light, and the third one flared, almost scorching her fingers. She lifted the glass chimney from the oil lamp and touched the match to the wick. The flame sputtered and took hold.

Carefully she set the chimney back on the base. The oil burned with a warm light that was nicer than an electric bulb, she assured herself. No need to worry.

A few minutes later the storm began to fade. Rain continued to beat against the windows, but the time between lightning flashes and the growl of thunder grew longer. Daisy turned on her side and drowsily watched the glowing wick.

The oil lamp flickered.

Instantly she was wide awake. The light had begun to tremble inside the glass chimney. She turned the switch that Gerald had said would raise the wick, and the flame shot upward, filling the chimney. *Too high!* she told herself, and turned it back. The light softened and was steady again.

But something had changed. She felt the difference before she saw what it was. On the opposite wall, between the chest of drawers and the closet door, a shadow hovered. It was a tall, hooded shape, slightly bent. As she stared, the figure glided toward the door. Panicked, she looked around, half-expecting to find a ghostly visitor beside the bed, but the room was empty.

When the shadow reached the door it stopped. Then it turned, and she imagined she could hear the swish of a robe as the figure slid back along the wall. At the foot of her bed, it stopped and seemed to turn again.

It was staring at her.

"Go away!" Her lips were stiff. The shadow moved back toward the door. Twice more it crossed the wall, stopping each time opposite her bed. Then, when she thought she couldn't bear this silent horror for another second, a humming began in a distant part of the house. There was a click, and the bedside light came on, flooding the room with light.

Daisy reached for the oil-lamp switch and twisted it hard. The flame vanished, taking the shadow with it.

"Everything okay in there, Daisy?" It was Gerald in the hallway. "I've got the generator going, and it looks as if the worst of the storm is over."

Daisy stared at the wall. How could she tell him—or anyone—what she'd just seen?

"I'm okay," she said shakily.

"Keep the light on if it makes you feel better,"

Gerald said. She heard his footsteps going down the hall.

If it makes me feel better! She was close to tears. Five Chimneys was haunted! She knew it now, even if no one else did. Why had she told Marna she didn't want to go home?

Chapter Six

When Daisy pushed back the curtains the next morning, the sky was like blue silk and the lake was calm. Looking out at the sparkling, freshly washed world, she could almost believe that the previous night had been a terrible dream.

But it happened! I might have imagined the thing on the beach, but I didn't imagine the shadow. It had been right there on her bedroom wall, and it had been Uncle Morgan's lamp that made it appear. She pulled on shorts and a top and then picked up the lamp, determined to get it out of her room.

"Morning, Daisy." Gerald was just starting down the stairs. "What's the matter? Didn't that lamp work for you?"

Daisy gulped. "It worked fine," she stammered. "But I don't need it anymore. I'm going to put it back in Uncle Morgan's room."

Gerald cocked his head at her. "Suit yourself," he said mildly. "If we're lucky, we won't have another storm as bad as that one for a while."

The bedroom at the end of the hall was as forbidding as Daisy remembered it, in spite of the bars of sunlight that stretched across the carpet. She tiptoed to the mantel and set the lamp back where Gerald had found it. A quick glance at the portrait made her cringe. Morgan Trier seemed to be watching her with a cruel little smile she hadn't noticed before. She hurried out of the room.

Downstairs, the Graveses were just starting breakfast.

"I adore the way everything shines after a storm, don't you, Daisy?" Trish greeted her gaily.

"You may not adore it so much when I tell you the roof is leaking," Gerald commented. "And I'm going to have to put in a new piling at the end of the pier. The storm split one of them—it must have been rotted part way through."

Trish's pretty face clouded. "Oh, dear, you'll have to work in that icy water," she moaned. "I'll help."

"Not in the water," he told her. "But you can hand me tools if you want. And say encouraging things."

Marna snorted. She shoved a cereal box in Daisy's direction.

"I'll help, too," Patty shouted. "I'll go in the water. I don't care if it's cold."

Trish put an arm around the little girl's shoulders. "Gerald and I will manage just fine," she said. She looked thoughtful, and Daisy guessed she was trying to think of a way to keep Patty busy while the piling was being replaced.

"I have an idea! Why don't you show Daisy your special trail this morning. I bet she doesn't know anyone else who has a forest trail all her own."

"It's nothing much," Marna muttered under her breath. But Patty was delighted, and as soon as she had finished eating, Patty found Daisy's hand and pulled her to the kitchen door.

This time, instead of heading toward the beach, they crossed the lawn on the north side of the house. When they reached the woods, Patty turned impatiently to Marna, who was several steps behind them.

"Where does it start?" she demanded. "Show me, Marna. And then let me be the leader. It's my trail."

Looking bored, Marna guided her sister to a birch tree next to a narrow opening through the trees. A sturdy rope was wrapped around the trunk and stapled in place. She put Patty's hand on the rope and stepped back.

"Okay," she said. "You're on your own."

Patty fingered the rope for a moment, then plunged through the opening into the woods. Daisy saw that the rope had been stretched from one tree to another. Brush and fallen logs had been pushed to one side to clear a path. Overhanging branches had been cut back.

"Who did all this?" Daisy asked Marna, as they hurried to keep up with the small figure ahead of them. "It's really cool."

"Gerald did it," Marna replied disdainfully. "He's always getting bright ideas."

The rope path angled to the left and sloped downward to the bank of a narrow stream. The water was only a few inches deep, and large flat stones had been arranged to make a bridge from one side to the other. Here the rope was stretched tightly, and again it had been wrapped and stapled to a tree on the other side. Patty crossed easily.

"Isn't this fun?" she called over her shoulder. "Don't be afraid, Daisy."

"Afraid, for pete's sake." Marna crouched down on the bank and waited for Daisy to cross. "Let's stop here for a while," she said. "Sometimes there are fish in this stream. You can go ahead, if you want to," she called to Patty. "We'll catch up."

Daisy hesitated. "Shouldn't we stay close to her? What if—"

"Doing something by herself is the whole idea," Marna snapped. "It's good for her. Ask Gerald—he's the big know-it-all expert. Besides," she added, "the rope starts curving back this way pretty soon. It forms a semi-circle and ends in our yard across from the back porch. She can't get lost."

Daisy hunkered down beside the glittering water. The stream made a whispery sound as it found its way between the stepping-stones. The air smelled sweet, and birdsong she hadn't noticed before was suddenly all around them.

This is what Patty knows about the woods, she thought. She could smell it and hear it and touch it. With the rope trail, she could enjoy it all without depending on anyone else.

"Gerald's nice," Daisy said impulsively. "Clearing the path must have been a lot of work."

Marna ignored the comment. "Look, there's a bunch

of fish." She leaned forward and put a stubby finger into the water. The school of tiny swimmers darted off.

Daisy stood up. She was uneasy with Patty out of sight. "Come on," she coaxed. "Let's see the rest of the path."

"If you want to." Marna dropped a twig in the stream and watched it float away. "Maybe I can get my mother to take us into town soon," she said as they followed the rope up the bank. "We can rent some videos, and there are stores . . ." Her voice trailed off, and she stopped walking so suddenly that Daisy almost bumped into her.

"Something's wrong!" Marna pointed at the rope, which now angled sharply to the right. "Patty!"

"What is it?" Daisy asked. "What's happened?"

Instead of answering, Marna began to run. She shouted her sister's name as she stumbled through the woods.

Daisy followed, stumbling herself, aware that the path was no longer smooth and easy to follow. The rope continued to curve to the right. When she looked up at the sun, she realized they were heading east. Toward the cliffs. Toward the lake.

"Patty, stop where you are!" Marna cried. "Stop, right now!"

"I'm stopped," called a small voice. "Hurry up!"

Marna fell over a tree root and scrambled to her feet. Tears streamed down her cheeks.

"She's okay," Daisy said. "She's waiting for us."

Marna didn't seem to hear. She pushed aside a low branch and let it swing back to hit Daisy a stinging blow on the forehead.

When Daisy caught her breath, she saw the end of the rope lying among fallen leaves a few feet ahead of them. Patty was crouched close to it, hugging her knees.

"Something happened to the path," she said mournfully. "I kept falling over stuff and then the rope stopped. So I sat down."

"You should have stopped the first time you fell," Marna scolded, her voice shaking. "You should have waited for us."

Patty looked surprised. "Are you crying?"

"Of course not," Marna lied. "Stay where you are for a minute."

She turned and motioned Daisy to follow her. They climbed over a log and continued on another few feet. When they stopped, they were at the edge of the cliff that overlooked the beach.

Daisy gasped. "She could have gone right over," she whispered. "She could have—"

"She could have been killed, that's what!" Marna's face twisted. "He did it on purpose!"

"Who did it?" Daisy thought of the threatening shadow on her bedroom wall. "Who do you mean?"

"Gerald, of course," Marna hissed. "The trail was his idea in the first place, and he's the one who changed it. He'd like to get rid of Patty and me—and my mom, too. All he cares about is Five Chimneys. I hate him!"

Chapter Seven

"Daisy, your mother's on the phone!"

Trish was waiting on the back porch when the three girls came out of the woods. Daisy was last, still stunned at Marna's furious accusation. When Trish called again, she began to run.

"Take the phone upstairs to your room if you want to." Trish's smile faded as she watched Marna and Patty cross the lawn, hand in hand. "What's wrong?" she asked, but Daisy had already snatched up the cordless phone and headed for the stairs.

"Daisy, how are you? Are you having a good time?" Her mother's voice was warm and comforting.

"I'm okay." Daisy went into her bedroom and closed the door behind her. "Where are you, Mom?"

"At JFK in New York," her mother said excitedly. "I'm on my way to London in about twenty minutes. I'd planned to call you from home, but our flight time was moved up, and I didn't have a chance to call. I'll be in London for the next week, I think."

"Oh." Daisy fell back on the bed, her feet dangling over the side. "Do I have to stay here till you get back?"

"Well, of course you'll stay there, hon." Her mother sounded surprised. "Mrs. Graves said you were having a good time. Is anything wrong?"

Daisy didn't know where to begin. The shadow, Marna's moodiness, the horrifying thing that had just happened in the woods . . . What good would it do to tell all that? Her mother was flying to London in twenty minutes!

"Daisy, what is it?"

"There's just a lot of stuff going on here," Daisy said. "I wish we were in Colorado."

"Well, so do I, dear!" her mother exclaimed. "And it won't be long before we're on our way. I've told Mrs. Graves where I'll be, and she says you're more than welcome to stay with them till I get back. Guess what? She says you're a joy to have around!"

A door banged downstairs. Daisy sat up and, phone in hand, went to the window. Trish was crossing the lawn to the beach steps, walking fast. The sound of hammering drifted up from the pier.

"That's nice," Daisy said absently.

"I'll call again from London, dear. If you want to get in touch with me, Mrs. Graves has a number."

"Okay. Have a good trip." Daisy didn't want to hang up. "I miss you, Mom."

"I miss you, too. Talk to you soon, hon."

She was gone. Daisy tried to picture the airport terminal, with hundreds of people milling around. The scene could hardly be more different from the view below her window—wide green lawn, woods pressing in on either side, the long stretch of beach below. She wondered if her mother believed in ghosts.

Downstairs, she discovered Patty alone in the kitchen, eating a peanut butter sandwich and looking unhappy.

"Mama's talking to Gerald and Marna's gone off somewhere," she said solemnly. "I think Marna's mad at me."

Daisy gave her a hug. "Why should she be mad at you?"

"Because I kept walking when I should have stopped," Patty explained. "I thought it was going to be all right. The trail's always been easy before."

"It wasn't your fault," Daisy assured her. "Somebody—some bad person found the rope and decided to play a trick. A trick on all of us," she added quickly, "not just you."

Patty nodded. "Mom says I can't walk there alone anymore," she said. "Not until we find out who else is using our woods."

"Good idea." Daisy glanced out the window in time to see Trish and Gerald crossing the lawn to the tree that marked the starting point for Patty's trail. "Your folks are going to look at the rope and try to figure out what happened right now," she reported. "Do you want to play the Detective game for a while?"

Patty decided to have a tea party with her dolls instead. Daisy helped her get settled in the living room, then wandered into the little library at the end of the hall. She'd thought Marna might be there, but the room was empty.

She looked at the bookshelves. There were dusty volumes of history and biography, and a whole row of guides to trees, flowers, rocks, and freshwater fish. Another shelf held bright-colored paperbacks, most of them fairly new. *They must be Trish's,* Daisy decided. The other books had probably been on the shelves when the family moved to Five Chimneys. She wondered which ones had been Uncle Morgan's favorites.

There was one, smaller than the others, that had no lettering on its spine. Daisy flipped it open and discovered it wasn't a real book at all, but a diary. *Property of Thomas P. Trier* was inscribed in neat, old-fashioned handwriting in the middle of the first page. *Thomas must have been Marna's grandfather,* she thought—the younger brother who had left Five Chimneys when Morgan died and had never come back. Was it all right to look into someone's diary if it had been left on a shelf where others could find it? She decided it was, and settled into a chair to read.

July 15, 1947

In the nineties today, and no relief in sight. I've decided to start a journal for one reason—I have no one to talk to. Morgan doesn't care to chat, and he has no interest in our business affairs. He expects me to make all financial decisions—wisely, of course. I'm not really complaining; he can't help the way he is. The land itself is all that matters to him.

There were footsteps in the hall. Daisy closed the diary guiltily as Marna appeared at the door.

"Don't bother to read that dull old thing," Marna told her bluntly. "I looked at it during Easter vacation, and it's all about selling lumber and stocks and fixing up the house." She held out the book she was carrying, and Daisy saw that it was the one she'd taken from Uncle Morgan's bedroom. "This one's a lot more interesting," she said with a sly smile.

"Not to me."

"You don't believe in spells," Marna said. "But I do. I practiced saying some of them last night, and it wasn't as hard as it looked. If I can make a spell work, everything's going to change around here. My mom won't listen to me, and my dad is too far away to help, so I have to do it myself. I'm going to get rid of Gerald before he murders us all."

Chapter Eight

"Gerald's sick," Trish said the following morning. "He's flat in bed with a fever and cough. And I'm not a bit surprised." She looked tired and worried. "He was in and out of the lake almost all day yesterday working on that piling. And he wouldn't let me help at all."

Daisy glanced at Marna, who appeared startled at first, then triumphant.

"Today of all days!" Trish went on. "He had such a nice surprise for you, Patty. He'd planned to save it until the water warms up, but after what happened yesterday he decided you needed something fun to do now."

"What is it?" Patty demanded. "I'm going to ask him if I can have it right away." She started for the stairs, but her mother caught her arm and stopped her.

"He's sleeping, and we're not going to wake him," she said firmly. "I only told you because it's good to have something to look forward to. Marna mentioned that she'd tied a rope around your waist so you could go in the water, but this is going to be safer, and it'll give you more freedom, too. Gerald's made a little harness you can wear with a long length of bungee cord fastened to it. You'll be able to wade or float or practice swimming without worrying about going out too far."

Patty's face glowed. "*Please* let's wake him up," she begged.

Trish shook her head. "Even if he were awake, I wouldn't let you try it until he was there to show you how it works, sweetie. I'm sorry I mentioned it. Come on, let's go down to the pier."

"I'd rather read," Marna said at once. But when the others headed out the front door, she trailed along.

"Now do you believe in spells?" she whispered when Trish and Patty were a safe distance ahead. "Yesterday I recited a whole bunch of them in Uncle Morgan's bedroom, and today Gerald is sick. They worked!"

"You didn't do it." Daisy's eyes were on the far end of the beach where the woods met the shore. "Gerald has a cold—you heard what your mom said."

Marna ignored her. "He's never going to have a chance to put that stupid bungee cord on Patty," she said smugly. "I bet he's fixed it so it will fall off while she's swimming."

"That's crazy!" Daisy exclaimed. But in spite of herself, she pictured the trail rope lying on the ground with Patty beside it, only a few feet from the edge of the cliff. Someone had turned Patty's trail into a deadly trap. If it wasn't Gerald, who could it have been?

Dinner that night was dreary, even though Trish reported that Gerald's fever was down and he was starting to feel better. Afterward Daisy and Marna cleared the table and washed the dishes while Trish played a game with Patty. Then they watched television, with Trish explaining to Patty what was happening in the places where the sound didn't make it clear.

No one bothered to build a fire, and as the evening wore on the living room grew chilly.

"I have the shivers," Patty announced suddenly. "Is the front door open?"

"No, it's not," Trish said. She touched Patty's forehead. "I hope you aren't coming down with Gerald's flu."

"She isn't," Marna said, her eyes on the television screen. "He had something special."

"Just the same, I think you should go up to bed, Patty," Trish decided. "I think we all should. If there's a flu bug going around, we can use some extra rest."

Daisy jumped up. Was it her imagination that made the living room seem colder every minute? Fifteen minutes later, snug in bed, with the bedside light on and the curtains pulled against the dark, she was still shivering. Thoughts of the shadow, the rope trail, Gerald's illness—all the events of the last few days whirled in her head. She closed her eyes and took slow, deep breaths, but she couldn't fall asleep. There was just too much to think about.

Finally she sat up and reached for Thomas Trier's journal. She'd brought it upstairs yesterday, deciding to see for herself if it was all as dull as Marna had said it was. Surely there had to be something interesting to write about if you were sharing a house with a wizard—even one who didn't like to talk.

She plumped up the bed pillows and settled back, turning the pages of the book slowly at first, then faster. It *was* dull. Whole pages discussed buying and selling stock, and there were detailed records of lumber sales. In the first twenty pages she found only a couple more lines about Thomas's older brother:

> Morgan was in an ugly mood this morning, raging against the enemies only he sees. He grew calmer as the day passed. . . .

Thomas had left space above and below that sentence, as though it had special importance. A few pages later, another entry was set off in the same way:

> Morgan stayed in the woods all day. He's begun to call the estate his kingdom—a harmless fantasy, I suppose, but he patrols constantly to be sure there are no "invaders." When he returns, his eyes are wild and his temper is vicious. Tonight he said he wants to put up a fence to keep out "spies." A ridiculous idea—I can only hope he forgets it by tomorrow.

The next couple of pages described repairs Thomas was making on one of the chimneys. Daisy yawned over the list of supplies needed—bricks, mortar, a new ladder.

Then she turned another page, and her drooping eyelids sprang open.

A dreadful day.

The handwriting was different here, ragged and hard to read.

John Caspar, the farmer whose land is next to ours, appeared at the back door in a rage this afternoon. He says his little boys were playing in our woods when Morgan leaped out at them in that robe he likes to wear. John claims he threatened the boys with a stick and told them they would die if they ever stepped on his property again. I tried to assure him Morgan wouldn't actually hurt anyone, but he didn't believe me. He said I should have put Morgan in a hospital for the insane long ago. He said if anything happens to his boys, he will hold me directly responsible.

I doubt I'll sleep tonight.

Daisy closed the journal. *Morgan's kingdom*, she thought with a shudder. Five Chimneys and the land around it were his property, where no one else was allowed. She dropped the book on the floor beside the bed, knowing that the thought of Morgan Trier patrolling his kingdom was going to keep her awake just as it had his brother.

Chapter Nine

"I think I'm going to live!" Gerald announced at breakfast. He grinned at Marna, as if he guessed this might not be what she wanted to hear. Then he winked at Daisy. "Two glasses of orange juice, three eggs, and a bagel—that ought to get me on my feet again, don't you think?"

"I hope so," Daisy said sincerely. She was tremendously relieved to see him at his usual place at the table. Trish looked much happier, too, and Patty was bursting with excitement.

"I'm going swimming!" she told Daisy, her face shining. "Gerald's going to show me."

"You know you can't go in the water right after breakfast," Trish reminded her. "Maybe if you wait till later in the morning the water will be a tiny bit warmer."

"And meanwhile, I'll cut the grass," Gerald said.

"Riding around on the tractor mower is about as much work as I'm ready for." He turned to Marna. "What are you girls going to do?"

Marna, hunched over her plate, pretended not to hear.

"Marna!" Trish sounded impatient.

"I don't *know* what we're going to do," Marna huffed. "There's nothing to do around here."

"How about some fishing?" Gerald suggested cheerfully. "Have you shown Daisy our pond? I can fix you up with rods, and maybe you can catch our dinner."

Marna scowled. "I hate fishing. It's the most boring thing in the whole world."

"I didn't know you had a pond," Daisy said quickly. "Where is it?"

"You have to walk back along the road we took in from the highway," Trish said. "Patty and I will show you if Marna doesn't want to."

"I didn't say I wouldn't show her the pond," Marna grumbled. "I said I hate fishing."

They finished breakfast in silence. Even Patty looked somber. Daisy could hardly wait until the table had been cleared and she could escape to the yard. When Marna joined her, they started up the road, not looking at each other.

"I wasn't mad at *you*," Marna said after a while. "I just don't see why we should fish because Gerald wants us to."

"But he didn't say he wanted us to," Daisy protested. "I think he was being nice."

Marna sniffed disgustedly. "It's in there," she said, pointing down a narrow trail that led off to the left. "Beyond those trees."

·They cut across a field littered with ancient stumps and entered the woods on the other side. Daisy followed closely at Marna's heels along the curving path.

The pond was bigger than Daisy had expected. The still water was the same dull silver as the sky, and birch trees and firs crowded close to the shore, except for a small open space where a rickety pier jutted a foot above the water. A boat lay upside down on the sloping bank.

"Do you want to take a ride?" Marna asked. "You can row if you want to."

"I don't know how," Daisy admitted.

Marna looked pleased. "I'll teach you. It's easy."

Together they turned the boat over and shoved it into the water, close to the pier.

"Be careful how you get in," Marna warned, then set the boat rocking herself as she jumped aboard. Daisy waited for it to steady before she settled in the back.

"Now watch me," Marna instructed. The prow of the boat swung out and back again as she pulled hard on one oar, then the other. Daisy gripped the pier with one hand and urged the boat out into open water.

"Okay," Marna said. "Now you have to dip the oars just right. Deep enough, like this, but not too deep." The tip of one oar skittered across the surface of the water, sending a shower over Daisy's head.

"Sorry."

"It scared the flies away." Daisy smiled. Marna might not have been very good at rowing, but at least she wasn't sulking. "How deep is the pond?"

"Not very. Except in the middle. It's no good for swimming though. Too many weeds."

"Do your folks own the pond, too?"

Marna nodded. "All the land back to the highway."

Morgan's kingdom. The words popped again into Daisy's mind, and at once the lonely gray pond seemed a dangerous place to be. She studied the shoreline with a feeling of dread.

"Oh!" She gasped and sat up straight.

Marna looked at her curiously. "What's the matter?"

"Look over there!" Daisy pointed.

Dropping the oars, Marna swung around to face the bow. "Where?" she demanded. "I don't see anything."

"R-right there," Daisy said through chattering teeth. "Someone's watching us. He . . . it's tall and thin and sort of . . . sort of *bony*. Look back in the shadow between those two big trees!" But as she spoke, the mysterious watcher slipped deeper into the woods.

"Where?" Marna demanded again. "There's nothing—"

"It's gone," Daisy said, "but I really saw it—" She broke off. Her feet were wet! When she looked down, she saw water pooling around her ankles.

"Marna!" She started to get up, then sat down again as the boat rocked. "The boat's leaking!"

Marna stared. Then she flung herself toward Daisy and reached behind her. "There's a plug back here," she sputtered, as water splashed her face. "It must have slipped out."

Under the girls' combined weight, the back of the boat sank lower. Daisy crouched to one side while Marna fumbled in the water.

"I can't find it!" she wailed. She scrambled back to the

oars and pulled hard on one of them, trying to turn the bow toward the pier. Water poured in over the side.

"We're going to sink." Daisy felt as if she were in the midst of a nightmare. "We have to swim back!"

Marna tried again to turn the boat. Another wave poured in.

"Come *on!*" Daisy knelt on the seat and half-tumbled, half-dived into the water. She clung to the side of the boat until a splash behind her told her Marna had jumped in, too. Then she began to swim.

It should have been easy. Daisy had always liked the water, and Marna, churning noisily behind her, didn't seem to be having any trouble. But swimming from a sinking boat was different from swimming for fun, Daisy discovered. The pier was farther away than she'd thought, and the water was very cold. She stopped long enough to kick off her sandals and looked back, just as the boat sank out of sight.

When she was only a few feet from the end of the pier, she tried to stand up. Weeds wrapped themselves around her legs, and her bare feet settled into muck. She kicked loose and began to swim again. A few more strokes and she was able to pull herself up on the pier. Marna stumbled to shore, clinging to the side of the pier, and threw herself on the bank.

Daisy dropped down beside her and propped herself on her elbows. An oar floated near the middle of the pond. "What did you mean about a plug?" she asked when she had caught her breath. "What kind of plug?"

Marna pushed dripping hair away from her face. "It's supposed to let out rainwater," she said. "If you leave the boat on shore, you can drain it before you use it again. We rowed around some when I was here at Easter, and Gerald checked the plug then." She sat up. "That's it! No wonder he wanted us to go fishing!"

More than ever, Daisy felt as if she were caught in a bad dream. "You don't really believe he loosened the plug," she protested. "You couldn't believe that."

"Sure I believe it," Marna retorted. "I told you he wanted to get rid of us, didn't I?"

Daisy sat up and stared across the pond at the shadowy place between two tall trees. "I think it's mean the way you talk about Gerald," she said bluntly. "He's not the only one who could have done it. And he's not the only one who could have changed Patty's trail, either. Someone else might want to hurt your family."

Marna followed her gaze. "No one was over there," she said. "Why would anybody else be in our woods?"

It's not your woods, Daisy thought. *It's your Great-uncle Morgan's woods. At least he thinks so.*

She was certain she was right. Marna's suspicions of Gerald were wrong and cruel, but it was true that someone wanted to make trouble for the Graves family. This time, Daisy had seen that someone clearly. And she was certain it was Morgan Trier's ghost.

Chapter Ten

The tractor mower was rumbling across the side lawn when the girls returned. Marna stopped at the end of the road, waiting for Gerald to see them, but his head was down, his face almost hidden by sunglasses and a visored cap.

"He knows we're here, all right," she muttered. "He just doesn't want to look at us. He was hoping we'd never come back."

"Can't you see he's busy?" Daisy snapped. She was tired of Marna's accusations, and she wanted to get out of her wet clothes. Most of all, she wanted to be by herself for a while.

She'd seen a ghost! She was sure of it, even if it hadn't looked the way ghosts were supposed to look— all pale and wispy. The *thing* she'd seen had been like a skeleton, yet not a skeleton. Its parts were oddly shaped, and it was huge—much larger than a man, even broader than the figure she'd glimpsed on the beach during the storm. *It's growing*, she thought. *And it hates us.* She had felt its hatred reaching out to them.

"What in the world!" Trish was shocked when the girls entered the kitchen, their wet clothes clinging, their hair in strings. When she heard what had happened, she hugged them tearfully and said she was *glad* the boat was at the bottom of the pond.

"I'd never have another peaceful moment if I thought someone might try to use it again!" she exclaimed. "I can't imagine what happened!"

"I can," Marna said, and stomped down the hall to the stairs.

Trish watched her. Then she hugged Daisy again.

"I'm so sorry, dear!" she exclaimed. "You're having a perfectly dreadful time, aren't you? What would your mother say if she knew you'd almost drowned!"

"We didn't almost drown," Daisy assured her. "The pond isn't that big, and besides, we can both swim. I'm just cold and tired and—"

"You go upstairs this minute and change," Trish ordered. "Lie down for a while, too. We'll do something special this afternoon to make up for your miserable morning. That's a promise!"

But Daisy didn't feel like lying down. When she'd changed into dry clothes, she wandered restlessly around her bedroom trying to make sense of what had happened. Finally she opened Thomas Trier's diary and curled up with it at the foot of the bed. A breeze lifted the curtains, bringing with it the drone of the mower as it moved back and forth across the grass.

She turned the pages of the diary, skimming over comments about the weather, more stock purchases, the sale of a large number of trees. It was several minutes before she came upon another mention of Morgan. Once again, the entry was set apart with extra space above and below it.

I went into town this morning and telephoned the doctor who signed Morgan's army discharge papers. He repeated the same things he said the last time I talked to him. Morgan's breakdown when he was in the army was serious, and his condition can't be cured. If he takes his medicine every day and doesn't get upset, he should be able to function. That's easy for the doctor to say, but how can I be sure he takes his pills? I am just the "little brother," as he often reminds me. His spells of rage are becoming more frequent, and he spends much time alone. I get no thanks for staying here with him. He thinks we are the most fortunate of men to have inherited this house and land and enough money so we don't have to go into the world to work. It never occurs to him that I stay for only one reason—I'm afraid of what terrible thing might happen if I were to leave him alone!

Sometimes he hides in his room for hours mumbling to himself—nonsense, mostly. Other times he tears out of the house in that ridiculous robe and vanishes into the woods for hours. I worry constantly that he'll run into someone again—a hunter or a hiker—and have another of his tantrums. When I warn him to be careful, he tells me I'm blind to the evil around us, and he will protect his kingdom at all costs. . . .

"Daisy, are you sleeping?"

Daisy closed the diary and slipped it under her pillow. Out in the hallway, Patty waited in a red-and-white swimsuit. "I'm going swimming!" she exclaimed. "You can watch if you want to."

"What about Marna?" Daisy looked past Patty at the closed door across the hall.

"I think she's sleeping," Patty said cautiously. "Anyway, Mama said not to bother her." She found Daisy's hand and gave a little skip. "I wish I'd gone with you to the pond. I've never been shipwrecked."

"Well, I'm glad you weren't there," Daisy told her. It was frightening to think of Patty flailing around in the water, not sure where the shore was.

They went outside and found the mower stopped in the center of the front lawn. Gerald and Trish stood next to it, talking. Gerald's face was grave. He shook his head when he saw the girls.

"Trish has been telling me we've had another near-disaster," he said grimly. "I'm sorry, Daisy. You're going to wish you'd never come to Five Chimneys. Are you all right?"

Daisy told him she was fine.

"I can't understand how it happened," he went on. "I was out at the pond to look around about a week ago. The boat was lying on the bank right where we'd left it in April, and there was certainly nothing wrong with that plug when we used the boat then."

Daisy was glad Marna wasn't there to hear Gerald say he'd been at the pond a week ago. She would be more certain than ever that her stepfather had tampered with the drainage plug.

"Come on," Patty begged. "I want to swim."

Gerald's frown faded. "Right!" he said. "You girls go down to the beach and I'll get the harness. It's in the garage."

A few minutes later they were all at the water's edge, and Patty was trying to stand still while Gerald slipped leather straps around her shoulders and fastened them to another strap at the waist.

"The bungee cord can't slip out, can it?" Trish asked.

"Not a chance." Gerald gave the cord a tug and then took Patty's hand. "You go ahead and wade in, and I'll fasten the other end to a piling."

"Maybe one of us should hold the other end," Trish said nervously, "just this first time. We can always pull her back."

"No!" Patty shouted over her shoulder as she splashed into the water. "I don't *want* anybody to hold it. I don't *want* you to pull me back!"

Gerald hesitated, but when Trish didn't argue, he walked out on the pier and knelt next to a piling. Daisy followed and watched as he coiled the line around the metal pole and fastened it snugly.

"Don't you hold it!" Patty shouted again. She was up to her waist now in the water.

"We aren't," Gerald called back.

Abruptly, Patty threw herself facedown and started to kick. Seconds later she was on her feet again.

"Was I s-swimming?" Her teeth chattered with cold.

"You'll do better if you float first," Gerald called. "Just lie back and let your feet sort of drift up to the surface."

"I can wade out there and help her," Daisy offered. "It's easier if you have a hand under your back."

Gerald shook his head. "If she wants help she'll say so," he said. "I think she really wants to do this by herself."

For the next few minutes they watched while Patty tried again and again to lie back on the surface of the water. Each time she disappeared and came up gasping. Trish walked out on the pier to stand beside them. She looked proud as Patty tried to follow Gerald's shouted directions, but Daisy could tell she was concerned.

"That's enough," she said finally. "Patty, your lips are absolutely blue with cold. We're going to pull you in, sweetie."

"No!" Patty grasped the bungee cord at her waist with both hands. "I know the way by myself, see? I can do it!"

They watched as she waded slowly toward the pier. Her lips *were* blue, Daisy saw, but they were curved in a proud smile. When she reached the pier, Gerald swung her up into her mother's arms and unbuckled the harness.

"You did fine, honey," Trish said. "Now we have to

get you warmed up fast. You can try again when it's warmer." She set Patty on her feet and led her along the pier. Daisy started to follow.

"Daisy?" Gerald was unfastening the cord from the pier. "Just a sec. There's something I want to tell you." He gathered the cord into loops. "Patty's a brave little girl, and we want her to try anything she wants. But not this—" he nodded at the bungee cord. "Not ever, unless I'm around, okay?"

Daisy nodded.

"We don't need any more accidents, do we?" He watched her closely.

Daisy was startled. Did Gerald think she was the troublemaker?

He smiled, as if he'd guessed her thoughts. "What I mean is, you're a sensible girl. I'd like you to sort of keep an eye on things when you kids are together. If you see something that worries you, tell me right away."

Then Daisy understood. Gerald didn't suspect her; he suspected Marna, just as Marna suspected him.

She nodded and mumbled, "Okay." As they walked up to the house, she wished she could tell Gerald that she had suspicions, too—terrifying ones that had nothing to do with Marna. But when she looked up at his round, kind face, she couldn't find the words to tell him. Gerald thought she was sensible. If she told him what she suspected, he would be disappointed in her.

And he'd never believe her.

Chapter Eleven

"I think we should go to Wincona this afternoon," Trish announced after lunch. "A trip to town would be a nice change—I promised Daisy we'd do something special to make up for the dreadful morning she and Marna had."

"Me too," Patty shrilled. "Even if I wasn't shipwrecked, I'm going, too."

"And I'm heading back to bed," Gerald told them. "I don't think I'm as fully recovered as I thought I was."

"What about it, girls?" Trish said. "Are you interested in a little shopping?"

Daisy felt like cheering. She was more than ready to get away from Five Chimneys and its problems for a while. Marna, who hadn't spoken all through lunch, managed a quick nod.

"Wincona isn't much," she told Daisy sourly, as if

they were the only people at the table. "It doesn't even have a library. But you can send your mother a postcard if you want. And there's a Dairy Queen."

"I don't know my mom's address," Daisy said. "I could send a card to her newspaper, I guess, and they'd mail it to where she's staying in London."

She felt a little like an orphan, admitting she didn't know where her mother was. Trish reached across the table and patted her hand. "Just think of all she's going to have to tell you," she said. "You're lucky to have a mother who leads such an exciting life."

"I'd rather she'd stay home," Daisy replied honestly. "Like you."

Trish laughed. "Well, I'm certainly a stay-at-home. It takes all kinds of mothers, I guess—and daughters." She glanced at Marna. "I just wish mine could manage to smile once in a while."

Marna pushed back her chair. "Let's go if we're going," she said hurriedly.

☠

On the way into town, Daisy thought about what Trish had said. Maybe she really was lucky to have a mother who had an exciting job, but she didn't feel lucky. What she'd like was what Marna already had—a mom who stayed home and a little sister and a nice stepfather.

"You should have called me when you found out Gerald was going to do that stupid bungee-cord business," Marna muttered, her voice low so that her mother and Patty, in the front seat, couldn't hear.

"It wasn't stupid," Daisy retorted. "Patty loved it. It wasn't dangerous at all."

Marna looked unconvinced. "That's because you were watching," she said. "He couldn't take a chance."

She was hopeless, Daisy decided. It was a relief when the van turned onto Wincona's narrow main street, ending the conversation.

"I'll park here in the middle of the block," Trish said. "Patty and I will do some grocery shopping while you two look around. There's a gift shop and a video place and a souvenir store. And right around the corner there's a little white house where a lady sells marvelous homemade fudge. You can pick out a couple of videos and get some fudge for us to nibble on while we're watching them." She handed Marna a ten-dollar bill. "That should cover everything," she said. "Have a good time, and we'll meet you back here in an hour. We'll stop at the Dairy Queen on the way home."

To Daisy's surprise, Marna's mood changed as soon as they were alone.

"The gift shop's right across the street," she said. "I want to go there first because I'm going to get a present for Patty. I saw it when we were here at Easter break, but I didn't have enough money then. I've been saving part of my allowance."

"What kind of present?" Daisy asked, but Marna wouldn't tell.

"You'll see," she said. "Patty's going to love it."

They crossed to the gift shop, and while Daisy chose some notepaper for her mother, Marna hurried to the back of the store. When they met at the cash register, Marna carried a small square box.

"Hold out your hand," she said. She opened the box

and spilled a hard white ball into Daisy's palm. "Reach into that little hole and press the switch," she ordered.

Daisy did as she was told. Suddenly, the ball buzzed and vibrated as if it were alive.

"It's supposed to be for pets," Marna told her excitedly. "But the box says blind people can have fun with it, too. They can follow the sound."

"Are you sure?" Daisy asked doubtfully. "Has Patty tried it?"

"Of course not." Marna took the ball back and handed the box to the clerk. "I haven't told anybody about it. I wanted to buy it first. Gerald thinks he's the only one with good ideas. . . ."

Daisy sighed. Gerald again.

"You'll see," Marna said. "I know what Patty likes."

They left the gift shop and went to the souvenir store, where Daisy found a picture-postcard of the Lake Michigan shore—a long view of beach backed by low cliffs.

"I'll save it for my scrapbook," she said. "So I can remember what your beach is like."

"I'll get one, too," Marna said. "For my dad."

They spent a few minutes looking at the coffee mugs, stuffed animals, vases, and hand-carved toys that crowded the shelves. "Junk," Marna said, but she waited patiently while Daisy picked out a little wooden deer to take to Jane Rosenberg in the fall. Then they ambled down the street to the video store, threading their way between groups of vacationers.

"You can pick the movies," Marna said. "You're company." She took the white ball out of its box and turned it on and off, startling the other customers in the store, while Daisy made her choices. Once, ignoring the clerk's annoyed expression, she even rolled the ball down an aisle.

The fudge store was their last stop. Its owner, an enormous sweet-faced lady, greeted them as if they were old friends. Her living room was her "store," with a glass-covered counter where trays of fudge were displayed. Next to the counter was a card table that held a cash register and a plate of samples—dark, light, and white fudge, some with nuts and some without.

"We might have to try them all," Marna said slyly.

"Most folks do." The woman's brown eyes danced.

Marna giggled, and Daisy realized it was the first time she'd heard her classmate laugh. They tasted, pretended to argue so they would have to taste again, and finally made their choice—dark chocolate with walnuts. Daisy put the box of candy in the sack with her other purchases.

When they returned to the van, Trish was lifting bags of groceries into the back, and Patty clutched the string of a bright red helium balloon.

"I have a surprise you're going to like better than a balloon," Marna told her. "It's a present!"

"What is it?" Patty demanded. The balloon bobbed to the rear of the van and almost escaped. "Show me, Marna!"

Daisy watched anxiously as the little girl opened the box and took out the ball. She wondered if Marna's happy mood would vanish, as suddenly as it had appeared, if Patty didn't like her gift.

She needn't have worried. When the ball buzzed, Patty shouted with delight. All the way home she clutched it in one hand, turning the switch on and off, and balanced her ice cream cone in the other.

"We're all going to get pretty tired of that sound," Trish commented, but she smiled into the rearview mirror as she said it. "That was a very thoughtful gift, dear."

Marna's face grew pink with pleasure.

Back at Five Chimneys, the girls took turns rolling the ball across the kitchen floor. At first Patty missed it, reaching to the right as the ball scooted by on her left. But after a few tries, she was able to stop it almost every time. Trish cheered so loudly that Gerald came downstairs to see what was happening.

"Watch me!" Patty squealed. Marna rolled the ball again, and Patty caught it three times in a row.

"That's terrific!" Gerald said. "Good for you, Patty. You too, Marna. How'd you ever think of a thing like that?"

Marna shrugged, trying not to look pleased. "I knew she'd like it. And besides," she added meaningfully, "a ball is *safe*."

No one asked why she said "safe" in that special way, but Daisy remembered it later. She was upstairs at her bedroom window, watching the waves roll in under the darkening sky and thinking about the whole strange, mixed-up day. Below her, Patty sat in a lawn chair with her favorite doll. Her small fingers moved carefully, sorting the doll's clothes.

As Daisy watched, something streaked across the

lawn from the side of the house. It was the white ball. Patty dropped the doll and leaped up as it buzzed past her.

"I'll get it!" she shouted, and raced across the grass to crash headlong into the mower that had been left in the middle of the lawn.

Chapter Twelve

"I didn't do it!" Marna shouted. "I didn't!"

They were in the kitchen, except for Patty, who lay on the living-room couch, her face almost as white as the bandage that covered the cut on her forehead.

"Keep your voice down, Marna," Trish said sharply. "No one's accusing you. But someone rolled that ball without checking first to see where it might go. It certainly didn't take off by itself."

"No, it didn't!" Marna clenched her fists. "But I didn't do it, and Daisy was upstairs, so that leaves"—she turned on Gerald fiercely—"that leaves you! You hate me and you hate Patty!"

"That's enough, young lady," Trish interrupted. "Go up to your room and stay there till dinnertime."

"I'll stay there forever!" Marna stomped out of the kitchen and down the hall.

"Mama!" Patty called from the living room. "What's wrong?"

"Nothing. Everything's okay." Trish shook her head in despair as Marna's door slammed upstairs.

"You'd better sit with Patty for a while," Gerald said tiredly. "She must have a whopper of a headache."

When Trish had left, he slumped into a chair and buried his face in his hands as if he had a headache, too. "What a mess!" he groaned. "Daisy, are you sure you didn't see anybody take that ball outside?"

"Patty took it out in the backyard herself," Daisy told him. "She must have left it there when she came in to get her doll."

"But then who—"

"It just shot around the side of the house," Daisy told him. "Marna wouldn't do that. I know she gets mad, but she loves Patty. She'd never hurt her!"

Gerald sighed. "You're probably right," he said. "I certainly hope so. But I wouldn't do anything to hurt this family either. So, if it isn't Marna, and it isn't me, and it certainly isn't you or Trish, who's the troublemaker around here?"

Daisy swallowed hard. She thought of the creature she'd seen on the other side of the pond.

"What's the matter?" Gerald demanded. "Are you okay?"

"I was just wondering"— Daisy took a deep breath— "maybe there's someone else . . ."

"Someone else?" Gerald frowned. "We don't have any close neighbors, Daisy. And even if we did, why would one of them play ugly tricks on us? It doesn't make sense."

Daisy stared at him wordlessly. If he couldn't believe there might be a real person hanging around Five Chimneys, how could she ever convince him that the mischief-maker might be the ghost of an ugly-tempered great-uncle who didn't want anyone else to live in his "kingdom"?

☠

That evening Daisy's mother called, just as they were sitting down to dinner.

"Take the phone in the library," Trish suggested. "Just think, Patty. Daisy's mom is calling her from across the ocean!"

She tried to sound cheerful, but her face was drawn. It had taken another angry scene to get Marna out of her bedroom and downstairs for dinner. Now she sat glowering at her food, while Gerald cut Patty's pork chop into bite-sized pieces and Trish looked anxiously from one to another. Daisy was glad to escape.

"Mom!" She closed the door of the library and threw herself into a chair.

"How are you, dear?" Her mother sounded very far away. "I'm sorry I haven't called before, but I've been working long, long hours."

"I miss you," Daisy said. Her throat felt tight. "When will you be home?"

"Saturday, I hope. Maybe Sunday. No longer than that, I'm sure. Are you all right?"

"Well . . ." Daisy hesitated. "Everybody here has problems. Half the time Marna doesn't even talk."

Her mother groaned. "And I thought this was going to be fun for you! Can't you find out what's wrong?"

"I know what's wrong," Daisy said. "She hates her stepfather. And weird things keep happening."

"Like what, Daisy?" Her mother's voice was wary. "Are Mr. and Mrs. Graves kind to you?"

"Oh, sure, they're great." Daisy bit her lip. Now was her chance to talk about the ghost, but she couldn't do it. Her mother wouldn't laugh, but she would say there had to be another explanation. She'd probably ask to talk to Trish and Gerald, too, and then they would be more upset than ever.

"What kind of weird things do you mean?"

Daisy sighed. "I'll tell you when you get home," she said. "Don't worry."

"Look, Daisy." It was her mother's let's-stay-cool voice. "I'm sorry you're stuck in a bad situation, but you're a strong person. You can ride this out—maybe you can even figure out a way to help Marna. She sounds as if she needs it. And I'll be home in just a few more days."

"I know," Daisy said. "Are we still going to Colorado when you get back?"

"Definitely! You keep thinking about that."

"Okay."

"Love you, dear." There was a click at the other end of the line.

Daisy sat for a moment, not wanting to return to the silent table in the dining room. *Just a few more days*, her mother had promised. It felt like forever.

"I've kept your dinner warm, Daisy." Trish hurried out to the kitchen and returned with a plate. "Is your mother having an exciting time in London?"

"I forgot to ask," Daisy admitted. "She said she's working hard."

"Well, someday soon we'll read about it in the newspaper," Trish said. "And meanwhile, we're very glad to have you with us. I just hope our problems aren't making you too unhappy."

"I'm going to bed," Marna announced, pushing back her chair. "I think I'm getting pneumonia or something from nearly drowning!"

"You're not getting pneumonia," Trish said. "And you're not going to hide in your room all evening. You have a guest."

"That's okay," Daisy said. "I don't mind—"

"No." Trish sounded stern. "We've had enough of this nonsense."

"It's cool enough for a fire," Gerald suggested. "I'll bring in some wood while you take care of the dishes."

"We have videos," Daisy reminded them. It seemed a long time ago that she'd picked them out.

"That's right!" Trish exclaimed. "I'd forgotten. You girls decide which one we should watch tonight."

Marna said at once that she didn't care, and since Patty was half-asleep on the couch by the time they all settled in the living room, it was left to Daisy to choose.

"There's a comedy and a mystery," she said doubtfully. "Maybe the funny one?"

"Good idea," Gerald agreed. "We could definitely use some laughs around here." He poked the logs in the fireplace, sending up a burst of sparks, then settled back in his favorite chair. "A good movie and a plateful of fudge," he muttered. "Maybe that'll cheer us up."

It didn't. After fifteen minutes Daisy decided the movie wasn't funny after all. Or if it *was* funny, she wasn't in the mood to enjoy it. She found it hard to keep her eyes on the screen. When she looked around, what she saw was the bandage on Patty's forehead, Marna's scowl, and the row of dark windows beyond the circle of firelight.

Another quarter hour passed, and Gerald stood up and stretched. "Guess I'm not ready for a movie tonight after all," he said. "Too much to do down in the workshop."

Trish looked after him anxiously as he left the room. "Maybe I ought to help him," she murmured. "I don't think he should tire himself."

Left alone, Daisy and Marna stared glumly at the television screen. "At least the fudge is good." Marna spoke at last. "Not even Gerald can spoil it."

Daisy glanced at her quickly to see if she was making a joke, but, of course, she wasn't. A moment later something struck one of the windows with a sharp crack.

"Mama!" Patty sat up, startled out of sleep.

"Mama's downstairs," Marna said. "It's okay, Patty. It was just a bird hitting a window."

"Was the bird hurt?"

Marna hesitated. "Probably not. Birds fly into windows all the time."

"But it might be hurt," Patty insisted. "Let's go outside and look." She started to stand up and winced.

"Daisy and I will look," Marna said impatiently. "You stay there."

But Daisy shook her head. "It wasn't a bird," she said, trying to keep her voice steady. "It was a long, smooth piece of wood. I saw it."

"But it isn't even windy," Marna protested. "How could a piece of wood blow up and hit a window?" She stopped. "You're making that up, aren't you? You don't want to go outside because you're afraid of the dark."

Daisy didn't argue. The hair on the back of her neck prickled. "I'm going to bed," she said. She stooped to give Patty a quick hug and then headed for the stairs. "Don't go outside, Marna," she said over her shoulder. "It wasn't a bird."

Chapter Thirteen

He'd been right outside the window.

Daisy huddled under the covers and tried not to think about what might be roaming outside the house at this very minute. She had pulled the curtains, and the bedside lamp was lit, but she couldn't stop shaking.

The piece of wood she'd seen at the window must have been part of the weird ghost-monster that was Morgan Trier. He was growing bolder. Till now he'd skulked in the distance or around corners, playing his tricks when no was looking. Tonight he'd tried another kind of attack, and she was the only one who knew.

She remembered what her mother had said on the telephone: "Maybe you can help Marna." But to do that she'd have to convince the Graves family that it was a phantom who was trying to hurt them. Somehow, she'd have to make them see what she had seen.

When she finally fell asleep, she dreamed she was stumbling through the woods with the ghost of Morgan Trier lurching at her heels.

☠

The next afternoon was so hot that all three girls decided to go swimming, even if the water was still too cold for comfort. Trish sat on the pier and watched Patty splash about happily at the end of the bungee cord. Marna and Daisy swam laps, farther out, until their teeth chattered.

"You're good," Daisy said when they returned to the beach to warm up. "Too bad St. Elizabeth's doesn't have a pool. You could be on the team."

Marna looked pleased. "I'm not as fast as you are," she said. "Why do you keep looking up the beach all the time? There's nothing there but woods."

"I was just thinking maybe we ought to take a walk— to warm up."

"Okay," Marna agreed. "As soon as Patty gets tired of swimming. If she ever does."

"Let's do it now," Daisy said. She jumped to her feet. The wooded area at the far end of the beach was where she thought she'd seen the phantom during the storm. And it was in the woods, beyond the pond, that she had caught her first real glimpse of him. If Marna was going to see him, too, the woods at the end of the beach might be a good place to start looking.

They walked slowly, toes curling into the warm sand. Daisy picked up a few stones, but mostly she kept her eyes on the woods.

"My father lives on a beach in California that's a lot

wider and longer than this one," Marna confided suddenly. "If he can't move back here, I'm going out there to live with him. He's going to teach me how to surf."

"You're going to leave your mom and Patty?" Something moved among the trees ahead. Daisy narrowed her eyes, then let out her breath. It was only a shadow.

"Oh, they'll come, too," Marna said confidently. "Pretty soon my mother's going to see what a bad person Gerald is, and she won't want to be married to him anymore."

Daisy shivered in her clammy bathing suit. She ordered herself to keep walking, but she was becoming more uneasy with every step. The pier and Trish seemed far away.

"What's the matter?" Marna demanded. "Why are you stopping?"

Because he's watching us, Daisy thought. *I can feel it. He's waiting for us.* The certainty made her stomach turn over. Was it fair to trick Marna into confronting something she couldn't bear to look at herself?

Frantically, she searched for an excuse to end the walk. "Look, a hole in the cliff." She pointed. "Let's see what's in it."

Marna shrugged. "Who cares? Rocks and dust and a lot of creepy bugs, probably. Besides, it's too high."

"No, it isn't." Daisy scrambled up on a small pile of boulders at the foot of the cliff. The opening was about ten feet above her head. "There's lots of footholds," she coaxed. "Haven't you ever wanted to try mountain climbing?"

"No! What's the matter with you, Daisy? I thought you wanted to take a walk."

Daisy found a ledge wide enough to stand on. She stepped up on one foot and felt for fingerholds.

"I bet there are bats in there," Marna warned darkly. "Snakes, too."

Daisy found a second ledge, then a third that was so narrow Marna yelped in protest. "That's far enough! If you fall you could really hurt yourself."

Daisy slid her hands over the rock face. The opening in the cliff, a V-shaped gap about four feet wide at the bottom, was just inches above her head. She tensed her shoulders, bent her knees, and pulled herself up the way Mrs. Thorp had taught them in physical education class. Her chin cleared the floor of the opening, and she stared into the cave.

"You can't see anything." Marna sounded scornful and nervous. "It's too dark, isn't it?"

It *was* too dark. For long seconds Daisy hung there, her shoulders aching with tension. Then she let herself down, reaching carefully for the ledges she'd used before. She was grateful when Marna reached up and guided her feet.

"Thanks." Daisy looked toward the woods and then turned away fast. "Let's go back," she said unsteadily. "I have to go in the water once more to wash off the dust."

"I told you it was a dumb thing to do," Marna said. "Could you see *anything* in there?"

"Well, it's a real cave," Daisy said reluctantly, "not just a little hole. It gets bigger inside the opening. And there was some junk piled a little way back on one side."

"What kind of junk?"

"I don't know. You're right . . . it doesn't matter. I just wanted to see if I could get up there." She moved ahead of Marna, willing herself not to run.

"Are you sure the junk wasn't just rocks?"

"It could have been." Daisy walked faster. "Look, your mom and Patty are going back to the house."

"You're acting funny," Marna said, but she stopped arguing and followed Daisy back toward the pier.

Daisy pressed her lips together. In the seconds that she'd clung to the rock face, peering into the cave, the feeling of being watched had grown so strong that she'd almost panicked. *It was just a feeling,* she reminded herself unhappily, but it had been strong enough to drive her off.

If she kept running away like this, how was she ever going to prove to Marna or anyone else that Five Chimneys was haunted?

Chapter Fourteen

"What's the matter, Daisy?" Gerald asked at dinner that night. "You look awfully solemn." His eyes flicked a question in Marna's direction.

"I'm okay," Daisy said. "Just sleepy. All that swimming . . ."

"And climbing," Trish said. "I saw you, Daisy, dear. I can't think why you'd want to climb those cliffs. There's nothing at the top but wildflowers and more woods."

Daisy took so long to reply that even Patty stopped eating. "There's a cave in the cliff," she said finally. "I wanted to look inside."

Patty dropped her fork. "A cave? I've never been in a cave in my whole life."

"I don't remember a cave," Gerald said, frowning. "How far is it from the house?"

Daisy told him. "There's a pile of rocks below it, so

maybe it just opened up in the last couple of days. The storm could have loosened the rocks."

"Then it's dangerous!" Trish cried. "You mustn't go up there again, girls. That whole section of the cliff could be ready to collapse!"

"I don't want to, anyway," Marna said. "Who cares about a stupid old cave!"

"Very sensible," Gerald commented dryly. "You shouldn't have tried it, Daisy. That could have been another accident waiting to happen."

After dinner they all watched Trish's favorite game show on television—or pretended to watch. Daisy's eyes moved constantly from the screen to the darkness beyond the living-room windows. The beef stew she'd eaten settled like rock in her stomach.

"Daisy?" Trish turned down the television set as the show ended. "Why don't you go to bed early and get a good night's sleep?" She stood up. "Come on, I'll go up with you. I have to get something from my bedroom. I'll be right back," she added. "Marna, tell Patty what's happening on the screen."

Upstairs, Trish hesitated in the hall while Daisy switched on the light and pulled the curtains. Then she came into the bedroom and closed the door softly behind her.

"Daisy, I'm sorry about the unpleasantness around here. Marna's being difficult, but I'm hoping she'll get used to having a stepfather when she knows Gerald better." Her big blue eyes filled with tears. "She's probably told you her father is coming back someday, but that won't happen. You see, he was driving when the accident happened that took Patty's sight. It was a stormy night, and he was drunk. When he realized what he'd done, he couldn't face it. So he left us."

"But Marna said—"

"Marna knows what really happened," Trish explained. "She just doesn't want to believe it. I thought I should tell you that much, so you would understand her a little better. She doesn't make friends easily, but she admires you very much. She'd never say so, but I know you're the kind of person she'd like to be." Trish wiped her eyes as she turned away. "She's so angry—I just hope she doesn't do something she'll regret."

Daisy didn't know what to say. When Trish was gone, she undressed and climbed into bed, her head whirling. For the first time she understood the pain behind Marna's dark moods. She realized, too, that it wasn't just Gerald who thought Marna was causing the "accidents" of the past few days. Trish believed it as well.

They were wrong. Marna wouldn't hurt her family or herself. She probably wouldn't even hurt Gerald, unless you counted reciting some silly spells from a dusty book. Marna was just unhappy. And she was going to be more unhappy if someone didn't expose the real troublemaker at Five Chimneys.

Someone. Daisy groaned. *I'm the someone!*

She thought for a moment, then slipped out of bed and turned off the lamp. When she opened the curtains and sat close to the window, she could see most of the moonlit beach.

I'll watch until he comes, she told herself. *Then I'll wake up Gerald and Trish and Marna, so they can see him, too.*

It wasn't much of a plan, but it was better than just lying in bed feeling sorry for the Graves family and for herself.

Chapter Fifteen

When she woke, the lake glittered like glass in the first rays of the sun. Daisy stretched and winced; sleeping in a chair was hard on the neck! And all for nothing! If the ghost of Morgan Trier walked on the beach last night, he'd waited until she was sound asleep.

She stood up and wiggled her shoulder blades. The house was quiet. She imagined how Thomas Trier must have felt, waking up here long ago—perhaps in this very bedroom. Every morning he must have wished, as she did, that he were someplace else.

His diary still lay on the dresser. She'd glanced at it a couple of times since she'd discovered the long passage about Morgan, but Marna had been right—most of it was boring. Now she sank back in the chair, deciding to skim through it while she waited for the family to wake up.

Stock profits, repairs on some window frames—she

yawned and turned the pages. Here and there were small references to Morgan: "Brother spends too much time alone. . . ." "Morgan seldom speaks, and when he does he is harsh. . . ." "Today Brother was gone all day, roaming the woods. . . ." She hadn't seen these notes before because they weren't set apart, as the earlier comments had been.

Poor man, Daisy thought. *No matter what he was doing, he couldn't stop worrying about Morgan!*

A door creaked, and footsteps sounded on the stairs. Daisy started to close the diary, then opened it again when she caught a glimpse of a page scrawled in pencil near the back. The lines were crooked and smudged, unlike the rest of the book, but the handwriting was Thomas's:

I cannot bear this much longer.

The words were like a cry of pain. Daisy read them out loud, and suddenly she felt as if Thomas were there in the bedroom talking to her.

I try not to think about it, but I do believe Brother grows worse with each passing day. He says our kingdom is being besieged and vows he will defend it. When I suggest he see a doctor, he flies into the most terrifying rage. . . . Yesterday, a fellow came to the door asking for Morgan. He claimed to be a writer searching for interesting stories about rural Wisconsin. Someone had told him about "the wizard of

Five Chimneys," and he wanted an interview. A mad idea! I sent him away, but I fear he returned today while I was in the woods chopping firewood. When I came back to the house, Morgan was repairing the brick walk that leads to the beach steps. It is the first real work he has done in months, but when I thanked him, his face turned dark red, with an ominous expression I cannot describe. I asked if he felt sick, and he growled something about a spy. Then he looked up with a dreadful smile and said, "Don't worry, little brother. I sent the rascal packing."

Daisy turned the page, almost ripping it in her haste, but the paper on the other side was blank. There were no more entries in Thomas's diary.

☠

"Daisy, is that you?"

The kitchen was empty, and Trish's voice, calling from outside, sounded odd. Daisy ran to the open back door and saw Trish crouched on the bottom step of the porch.

"I took a silly tumble," she said through clenched teeth. "I'm afraid I've done something to my ankle. Would you fill a plastic bag with ice and bring it out here, sweetie?"

"Okay." Daisy hurried to the refrigerator and took out a tray of ice cubes. She had no idea where the plastic freezer bags were kept and was about to go back to the porch when Gerald appeared.

"What's going on, Daisy? Are you the cook today?"

"Trish fell and hurt her ankle," Daisy explained. "I need a plastic bag to make an ice pack."

He stared. "Hurt herself? Trish?"

"It's just my ankle," Trish called from outside. "Don't get in a state. The bags are in the second drawer next to the fridge, Daisy."

Gerald went outside, and Daisy followed a moment later with the ice pack and a towel to wrap around it.

"Oh, that's much better," Trish sighed, when the bag was fastened snugly in place. "I don't think it's broken, but it hurts! The ice will keep it from swelling and getting stiff."

"Can you stand up?" Gerald still seemed stunned. "We should get you inside. I'll carry you."

Trish forced a laugh. "Oh, no, you won't. A sprained ankle is bad enough—we don't need a sprained back, too. Besides, I'd rather stay here for a while. That's why I came out in the first place, to enjoy the birds."

"How did it happen?" Gerald demanded. "Where were you when you fell?"

Trish reached back and touched the second step.

He knelt to examine the board, and Trish gestured toward something lying on the ground, close by. It was a smooth piece of wood, about a foot long.

"Actually, that was lying on the step," she said reluctantly. "It's a piece of driftwood, I think. Someone— I guess Patty—carried it up from the beach."

Daisy stepped back. She felt cold, in spite of the sunlight.

Gerald shook his head. "Patty knows better than to leave stuff on stairs—for her own sake as well as other people's. I don't believe she'd do that." Daisy guessed what he was thinking.

Trish guessed, too. "It wasn't Marna, I'm sure," she said quickly. "What would Marna be doing with a chunk of driftwood?"

"Making trouble," Gerald retorted. "Not caring who gets hurt as long as she can spoil everybody's summer."

Trish looked up at him pleadingly. "It was just an accident, Gerald. We don't know who did it, so we mustn't accuse anyone."

"Accuse anyone of what?" Marna's question, from the other side of the screen door, made them all jump.

"Nothing," Trish said. "I've stumbled and twisted my ankle, that's all."

Marna opened the door and stepped outside. Patty was close behind her. "You fell?"

"I *slipped*," Trish said. "And if it's okay with all of you, I'm tired of talking about it." She reached up and pulled Patty down on the step beside her. "Why don't you girls put the breakfast things on the table? Gerald will help me inside when you're ready."

"I can do it all myself," Patty declared. She jumped up, and Daisy and Marna followed her into the kitchen.

"I bet Gerald pushed her," Marna whispered. "She doesn't want us to know."

"He didn't!" Daisy was indignant. "He came downstairs after I did."

"Well, I don't see what the big mystery is," Marna muttered. "Why doesn't she want to talk about it?"

Silently, Daisy took cereal bowls from the cupboard and handed them to Patty. The piece of driftwood had been narrow and smooth, like the object that had struck the living-room window. Another of Morgan Trier's ugly tricks!

I can't wait any longer, she thought desperately. *I have to tell someone now.*

Her chance came later that morning. Gerald had helped Trish out to a chair on the front lawn and propped her foot on a stool.

"I'll be in the workshop if you need me," he said, with a glance in Marna's direction. "Please be careful, everybody. We don't want any more problems."

Marna was rolling the vibrating ball for Patty to find. "Don't worry," she said. "Nothing's going to happen while *I'm* around."

Daisy waited a few minutes and then went into the house. She followed the sound of a radio down the basement stairs. Gerald was bent over a bookshelf, putting on a final coat of white paint.

"Hi." She wished she were a thousand miles away.

Gerald straightened up fast and laid the brush across the top of the paint can. "What's wrong, Daisy?"

"There's something I have to tell you."

"About Marna? What's she up to now?"

"She's not up to anything." Daisy took a deep breath. "Marna isn't trying to hurt people. There really is someone else." And then, talking fast so he couldn't interrupt, she told Gerald about the phantom.

"I know it sounds weird," she finished, the words tumbling over each other. "I've never believed in ghosts before, but I've seen him! He's real! I think he's made himself a kind of body because he wants to be as scary as possible."

96

Gerald blinked. *"Made himself a body?"*

Daisy nodded. "Out of driftwood and branches and . . . I don't know what. He's taller than you are. I'm sure it's Morgan Trier."

She waited for Gerald to say something.

"That's the strangest story I've ever heard, Daisy."

"I know."

"And I can tell you believe it," he went on. "I know you want to help us understand why we're having so many accidents."

"But they aren't accidents," Daisy said. She was close to tears.

"No, they aren't," Gerald agreed. "They couldn't all be accidents. You must have seen by now that Marna's unhappy because her mother and I are married. She's trying hard to spoil our life here. We have to stop her—but we won't do it by making up stories about a bad-tempered ghost. There has to be a better way than that."

"I'm not lying," Daisy said shakily. "I've seen him!"

She'd been afraid Gerald would laugh at her. Now she decided it would have been easier if he had. The look on his face was exactly like Miss Mackey's had been when she wrote the *D* on the story about the burglar.

"You're a good friend, Daisy," he said gently. "I hope Marna appreciates you. And one thing is true for sure—you have an amazing imagination!"

Chapter Sixteen

For the rest of the day Trish stayed off her injured foot, while Marna sulked and Daisy tried not to meet Gerald's eyes. She knew he was sorry he had hurt her feelings, but it didn't help. *Making up stories . . . an amazing imagination . . .* The words rang painfully in her ears.

"Somebody's mad at somebody," Patty murmured while they were eating breakfast the following morning, but she didn't ask for an explanation.

Why should she? Daisy thought bitterly. Somebody had been mad at somebody ever since she and Marna had arrived at Five Chimneys.

The girls spent the morning on the beach, helping Patty build a sand village, but at noon the sky darkened and the wind changed, driving them indoors. Daisy and Marna settled down with Monopoly in the living room, where Trish dozed on the couch. Patty stayed out on the narrow front porch playing school with her dolls.

"You're not even trying to win," Marna complained after they'd played for an hour. "You're making really dumb moves, Daisy."

"Marna, for goodness' sake!" Trish raised her head. "Do you have to be rude?"

"Well, it's true," Marna snapped. "And if Patty sings that A-B-C song once more I'm going to scream."

"What song?" Daisy asked. She'd been wondering how many hours had to drag by before her mother arrived back in Chicago.

"Just listen!" Marna exclaimed. "She's sung it to her dolls about a hundred times, can't you hear?"

Trish sighed. "Marna, please! We're all a little grumpy, Daisy, but things will get better." She closed her eyes again.

"She's asleep," Marna whispered after a moment. "Do you want to play or don't you?"

"Not much," Daisy admitted.

"Then I'm going to read," Marna said. "Upstairs." She swept the game pieces into the box and left the room without looking back.

Daisy stared at the cordless phone on the coffee table. *Ring!* She pleaded. *Get me out of this!* She imagined her mother's voice: *Good news, hon. I'm in Chicago! I'm coming to get you this afternoon!* But the phone remained stubbornly silent.

What could she do besides worry about what mischief Morgan Trier might try next? She remembered the row of paperback books in the library and wondered if she could find a story interesting enough to make her forget, for a while at least, how frightened she was.

Outside the library window a chickadee chirped. It was an anxious sound, as if the bird were worried, too. Patty's A-B-C song ended and began again as Daisy settled in a chair with a lapful of books.

At first she looked out the window every few minutes to study the woods that edged the lawn. Then she discovered that one of the books was about a fourteen-year-old pioneer girl who was left to care for her little brothers when their parents drowned in a flood.

"There was danger all around her," said the book's cover. Daisy knew how that felt. She leaned back and began to read.

She read fast, caught up at once in the story. Gradually, the light dimmed in the library. When footsteps sounded in the hall, she returned with a start from the lonely cabin in the forest where the pioneer girl was struggling to learn how to shoot her father's rifle.

"So there you are, Daisy," Gerald said cheerfully. "It was so quiet up here, I thought everyone had fallen asleep."

"Just Trish." Daisy tried to smile and failed. "Marna's up in her room."

"Where's Patty?"

"On the front porch, playing school."

Gerald's smile vanished. "No, she isn't."

"Sure she is," Daisy insisted. "I saw her just before I came in here." She glanced at her watch. Over two hours had passed. She had no idea when Patty had stopped singing.

"You check her bedroom," Gerald said tensely. "I'll look around the yard."

Daisy jumped up, spilling paperbacks from her lap.

"Quietly," Gerald warned. "We mustn't worry Trish."

Kicking off her shoes, Daisy hurried down the hall and up the stairs.

Patty's bedroom was empty, and neater than usual since she'd carried all her dolls downstairs to learn their A-B-C's. Heart thudding, Daisy tiptoed along the hall. She looked in all the other bedrooms, even Uncle Morgan's. When she reached Marna's closed door, she hesitated. There was no sound from the other side. *Better not get her excited*, Daisy decided. Patty might be back on the porch by now.

But when she went downstairs, one look at Gerald's face told her he hadn't found her.

"I've been all around the yard," he said. "We could check the rope trail, but I think it would be a waste of time. I doubt she'd even think of trying it again until we've found out who fooled around with the rope."

"Would she go swimming by herself?" The thought was so terrifying that Daisy could hardly get the words out. Gerald shook his head but started toward the stone steps leading to the beach. "She knows how dangerous that would be," he muttered.

Daisy had another idea. "She was pretty excited when Marna and I told you about finding that cave. Maybe she decided to look for it herself."

"How could she?" Gerald growled. But when they stepped out onto the sand, Daisy saw that she had guessed right. Far up on the beach Patty was crouched, a few feet from the pile of fallen rocks.

"What in the world!" Gerald sounded relieved and very angry. "What is she doing?"

Daisy remembered the morning she and Marna had raced along the rope trail to its end. "She's waiting for someone to come. She doesn't cry when she's scared—she just sort of curls up and waits."

They began to run. Daisy was faster, her bare feet flying over the wet sand. She was hugging Patty by the time Gerald caught up.

"Patty!" He was puffing hard. "What are you doing out here alone?"

"I went for a walk," Patty said, freeing herself from Daisy's arms. "I'm okay."

"But why? You know you're supposed to stay in the yard."

"I just wanted to find the cave myself," Patty said. Her voice shook a little. "Daisy said there was a pile of rocks in front of it, so I knew I could find it. I wasn't going to go *into* it," she added hurriedly. "I just wanted to climb up and reach inside."

Gerald seemed to notice the triangular opening above them for the first time. "Reach inside!" he repeated. "Good grief! What are we going to do with you?"

Patty put out her hand and he took it in both of his. "I didn't do it, so you shouldn't be angry," she said coaxingly. "I found the rocks, but then things kept getting in my way. Trees, or poles, or something. And when I tried to go home, I couldn't. They were there, too."

"Trees?" Daisy swallowed hard.

"There aren't any trees on the beach," Gerald said impatiently. "You're all mixed up, Patty. If you bumped into anything, it was rocks."

"Was not!" Patty stood up and pointed to an empty

space in front of the pile of fallen rocks. "It was those trees. Or whatever they are. I couldn't get past them." She tugged his hand. "Let's go home right now. I don't want to be here anymore. It feels funny."

As they started back along the beach, Daisy stole a quick glance at Gerald's face. She wondered if he was remembering how she'd described the ghost of Morgan Trier.

"There were, too, trees," Patty whispered under her breath. "I felt 'em."

"I believe you," Daisy said softly.

She didn't care if Gerald heard.

Chapter Seventeen

"I'm going to hire someone to seal up that cave first thing," Gerald said grimly. "It won't be there anymore, Patty, do you understand?"

The little girl nodded. She wore the same troubled expression she'd had the morning the rope trail had been changed. Her world had played another trick on her. Watching her, Daisy was not just afraid of Morgan Trier; she despised him, too. Patty couldn't afford to lose her hard-won confidence.

"We won't say anything about this to your mother," Gerald continued as they crossed the lawn to the house. "It would upset her if she knew you'd gone off by yourself like that. You won't do it again, will you?"

"No!" Patty settled herself on a porch step and cuddled a battered-looking baby doll. "Don't you ever run away," she told it. "If you do, something will *get* you!"

When they went into the house, Trish was sitting up on the couch with the phone on her lap.

"Daisy, you just missed a call from your mother." Her voice was strained. "She's flying home tomorrow, and she'll come to pick you up on Sunday. I told her we'd be happy to meet her halfway, but with this ankle—"

"It's worse, isn't it?" Gerald exclaimed. "I was afraid of that."

"It isn't any better," she admitted. "I think I should have a doctor look at it."

Gerald patted her shoulder. "We'll go to the clinic in Wincona right now," he said. "Daisy, will you run upstairs and get Marna?"

"She won't want to go," Trish protested. "She's in a bad mood, and you know she'll hate waiting around in a doctor's office. What about you, Daisy?"

Daisy hesitated. She couldn't stop thinking about what had just happened. She was certain it was the ghost of Morgan Trier that had barred Patty's way to the cave. He'd wanted to frighten her, and he'd succeeded. Maybe, Daisy thought uneasily, there was a special reason why he'd wanted to keep her away from the cave. If there was, this would be her last chance to find out what it was.

"You don't have to come with us, Daisy," Trish said. "Do whatever you want to do."

"I'll stay here, I guess."

"Well, Patty's coming," Gerald said sharply. "And you stay close to the house, Daisy. No expeditions."

"Expeditions?" Trish repeated. "What do you mean?"

"Nothing special," Gerald said. But he gave Daisy a long look as he helped Trish to her feet. *Don't start imagining things again*, the look warned, as clearly as if he'd spoken the words aloud.

Fifteen minutes later they were gone. Daisy stood at the library window and watched the car bounce along the narrow road and out of sight. For a moment she wished she'd gone with them. Then she remembered Patty's small, frightened face as she'd crouched in the sand. Morgan Trier had done that to her. He'd do it again if he had the chance.

She found a pad of paper and a pencil next to the telephone and scribbled a note for Marna, explaining where the family had gone. She added a few hasty lines at the end:

> I'm going out, but I'll be back in a few minutes. Your mom said we should have soup and sandwiches for supper.

She propped the note against a vase of wildflowers on the kitchen table, then searched through cupboard drawers until she found a flashlight. The sky was overcast, and even though it was still daylight, the cave would be dark. *Horribly dark!* she thought with a shiver. She knotted a length of twine around the flashlight's handle and then looped the twine around her neck. Now both hands would be free to climb.

I'll just take one quick look, she promised herself. She hoped Gerald wouldn't find out, but if he did, well, it was actually his fault she was going. He'd refused to believe what she'd told him about Morgan Trier. He had to have proof.

106

When she returned to the beach, the wind had died down. She moved fast, her eyes on the woods ahead. Now that she knew where the footholds were, maybe she'd be able to climb up to the cave more quickly this time.

As she walked, she began to feel again that she was being watched. The sensation grew stronger as she reached the rock pile, and for a moment she paused there, taking deep breaths. Then she climbed up on the rocks and reached for the first handhold to pull herself up.

Morgan Trier may be watching, but Patty's the only one he's ever come close to, she reminded herself. *He's a bully who picks on a little kid.* The thought gave her courage to move on.

Now she was at the point where she had been able to lift herself with both hands and look briefly into the cave. This time, though, she needed a higher foothold, so that she could keep one hand free to use the flashlight.

Cautiously, she examined the face of the cliff. The only ledge she could find was a very narrow one to the right of the opening.

I'll have to lean way over to see in, she thought unhappily. *It's too far!* But she had to try. If she hesitated now, she knew she would scramble straight down and run all the way back to the house.

A root stuck out from a crack above her, and she grasped it tightly as she stepped up and to the right. With her other hand she gripped the flashlight without removing the loop around her neck. Then she worked her way carefully along the ledge, until she was as close to the cave as she could get.

NO!

The voice was in her head—she knew that—but it cut through the stillness of the beach like a thunderbolt. She leaned toward the opening.

The beam of the flashlight made a bright hole in the dark as it danced over packed earth walls and a pebbly floor. It touched on the pile of rocks she'd seen before, on the far side of the opening. Daisy moved the beam slowly along its base, then stopped at a glint of metal. She swung the light up a little and saw another flash. There was something familiar about the shiny bits.

She braced the flashlight on the edge of the opening and studied one of the metal objects. A bicycle handlebar? The rubber grip was gone, and the metal was dented, but she was almost sure she was right. She tilted the beam toward the floor again. This piece of metal was curved, a reddish color. It looked like part of a bicycle fender.

A bicycle hidden in a cave! She stared at the pile of rocks and earth until the ache in her right arm forced her to shift her weight back to the ledge. For a few seconds she rested, pressing one cheek and then the other against the rock face while she scanned the beach. She was alone. Yet now, more than ever, she knew she was being watched.

She leaned toward the opening again.

GET OUT!

This time the voice in her head was a shriek. She jerked back, and a chunk of wood hurtled from the top of the cliff, barely missing her left shoulder. She clung to the root and bent her knees, trying desperately to find the ledge she'd used on her way up. Her toe settled on it just as a boulder as large as a basketball shot past her face and crashed on the rocks below. A smaller stone struck her shoulder, and she gasped in pain.

JUMP!

She pictured the rock pile below her and knew she could be badly hurt if she landed there. That was what Morgan Trier wanted! But if she could leap beyond it or to one side . . . She dropped her arms to her sides, turned around, and threw herself toward the sand and tall grass.

She landed on the balls of her feet and pitched forward, scraping knees and elbows in the sand. For a moment she lay stunned, unable to catch her breath. Something struck her foot, and when she looked down she saw a branch, the thickness of a broom handle, lying across her ankle. She scrambled to her feet and stared up at the top of the cliff. There was nothing above her except rock and gray sky. Then another branch tumbled over the edge, as if tossed from a distance by a clumsy hand.

☠

"Where were you?" Marna demanded. "I didn't even find your note till a minute ago. Why didn't you call me . . ." Her eyes widened as she saw Daisy's scrapes and bruises. "You went back to that cave, didn't you? And you fell!"

Daisy sank into a chair. She had run almost all the way back to the house.

"I wanted to look inside again," she panted. "Gerald's going to have it sealed up. He said so this afternoon." She described how Patty had gone exploring all by herself but left out the part about the "trees" that had blocked the way to the cave. "Gerald doesn't want your mother to know because she'd worry."

"She'd worry if she knew you went back there, too," Marna said gruffly. "So why did you? It's just a hole in the rock . . . isn't it?"

"I guess." Daisy knew that trying to tell Marna about the phantom would be a waste of time. She might pretend to believe in magic spells, but she'd sneer at the idea of a real ghost.

"You thought you saw something in there before," Marna prodded. "Did you find out what it was?"

Daisy sighed. "It's a bicycle," she said. "Most of it's buried, but that's what it is."

"A bicycle?" Marna repeated. "You saw a *bicycle*? I don't believe it!"

Daisy stood up. At that moment she was angrier than she'd ever been in her life. She hurt in a dozen different places, and if she described how she'd happened to fall, Marna wouldn't believe that either.

"I don't care what you believe!" she exclaimed. "I'm not even going to think about it anymore. You wouldn't believe the truth if . . . if it threw a rock at you!"

"What?" Marna looked baffled. "What are you talking about?"

"I'm going to take a bath and change my clothes and make a sandwich," Daisy said, heading for the stairs. "And then I'm going to watch television. And I'm not going to talk to *you* about anything!"

"Oh," Marna said, in an unexpectedly small voice. "Well, that's fine with me."

Chapter Eighteen

One more day. Daisy's eyes flew open. She thought she'd heard her mother's voice calling her up through layers of sleep. Tomorrow they would be together again, driving away from Five Chimneys. She could hardly wait, especially when she remembered the previous night.

It had been an awful evening. Trish had apologized and gone up to bed right after dinner. Her ankle was badly sprained but not broken, and the doctor in Wincona had given her pills to ease the pain and help her sleep. Patty had curled up in a chair in the living room with a doll and a teddy bear and had turned down Daisy's offer to play Detective. Her small face was pale, and a worry line had appeared between her eyebrows.

Gerald was quiet, too. Usually he went down to the workshop for a while after dinner, but last night he'd read and watched television all evening. Daisy guessed he didn't want to let Patty out of his sight.

Or maybe he didn't trust me, she thought unhappily. Trish had been too full of painkillers to notice that Daisy had changed from her shorts to slacks and a long-sleeved shirt, but Gerald had asked if she was cold. Had he guessed she was hiding bruises from a forbidden expedition? She hoped not, but she was sure of one thing: He might *say* Marna was lucky to have her for a friend, but he didn't mean it. He thought Daisy Gorman's imagination was making things worse, not better, at Five Chimneys. He'd be glad when she went home.

And then there was Marna. Daisy sat up and kicked off the covers. She didn't like to think about Marna. That stunned expression when Daisy had lost her temper— for a moment she'd looked as young as Patty and just as bewildered. All evening, as they sat side by side watching television, Daisy had kept remembering, guiltily, what Trish had confided two nights earlier:

Marna doesn't make friends easily, but she admires you very much. She'd never say so, but you're the kind of person she'd like to be.

She glanced at her watch. It was only five-thirty. The family wouldn't be up for a couple of hours. She wandered to a window and pushed back the curtains. In the first rays of the sun the beach looked like pale gold and the lawn sparkled with dew. It was pretty and peaceful.

For a moment she tried to make herself believe that Gerald was right: The phantom was a "made-up story about a bad-tempered ghost." She had never really *seen* that towering, ungainly figure. The accidents were just accidents. The rocks and sticks that had forced her from the cliff would have fallen whether she was there or not.

She wished she could believe all of it. She would leave the Graves family with a clear conscience if she could convince herself that Gerald was right and she was wrong.

With a sigh, she turned away from the window to make her bed and dress in yesterday's pants and shirt. Carrying her shoes, she tiptoed down the hall to the top of the stairs. Then she stopped, startled. Someone moved in the half-light below.

It was Marna. She'd been sitting on the floor, her chin resting on her knees. When she saw Daisy she scrambled to her feet and waited for her to come down.

"I knew you were going back there," she whispered. "I've been waiting for you."

Daisy stared at her. "Back where?"

"To the cave," Marna said impatiently. "I think that's very interesting—finding a bicycle in there. I really do. Maybe there's something else. I'll help you look."

"No way!" Daisy shook her head. "I got up because I couldn't sleep, that's all."

"It'll be easy this time," Marna continued eagerly. "Come on!" She opened the door and went out. Stunned, Daisy followed. This was a Marna she hadn't seen before.

When they reached the steps to the beach, Marna pointed. A ladder lay on the sand below them. "I dragged it all the way from the garage and let it slide down the steps," she explained proudly. "We can prop it against the cliff, and I'll hold it while you climb up. You can look as long as you want to."

"But we're not supposed to go there," Daisy argued. "It could be dangerous. Gerald said—"

"I don't care what he said," Marna interrupted. "And if I don't care, why should you? You're going home tomorrow. Anyway," she added, "you went there by yourself yesterday, so why shouldn't we both go now? We'll be back before anyone else gets up."

Daisy bit her lip. Marna didn't know why the cave might be important, but she wanted to prove she knew how to be a friend. A real friend tried to help, even if she didn't understand what was wrong.

Not like me, Daisy thought miserably. *All I want to do is jump in our car and ride away. A real friend would keep trying as long as she could.*

"Okay." She said it quickly, before she could change her mind. "Let's go!"

Chapter Nineteen

Daisy slipped into her shoes and ran down the stone steps, two at a time. The ladder was heavy, but Marna lifted the other end and they started up the beach, moving as fast as the sand would allow.

"We can slow down a little, Daisy," Marna protested, when they'd traveled half the distance to the cave. "It's still early."

Daisy's head pounded. Yesterday's bruises had begun to throb, but she walked faster. "We have to get there before he sees us," she told herself, and then realized that she'd spoken the words aloud.

"Before who sees us? Gerald? He's fast asleep."

Daisy didn't reply.

When they reached the cave, Marna sank down on the sand. Her face was flushed and shiny with sweat.

"Rest, Daisy," she begged. "Just for a minute."

But Daisy didn't dare stop. While they walked, she'd been on guard every minute, inspecting the beach and the grass-lined tops of the cliffs, dreading what she might see. Now, after one more look around, she dragged the ladder to the rocks below the mouth of the cave.

Marna groaned and got up to help. Together they raised the ladder over the rocks till the top rested a few inches above the floor of the opening.

"There!" Marna puffed. "Go ahead! I'll hold the bottom so it can't slip."

Daisy stepped up onto the first rung. The ladder shifted and dug into the sand. "It's all right," Marna assured her. "Keep going!"

She took another step, clinging so tightly that her fingers ached. The terror she'd felt yesterday had returned, stronger than ever. "Let me know if you want to go back," she whispered.

Marna scowled up at her. "Why would I want to do that?"

"You might see . . . somebody."

"Who would I see? I'm not afraid of Gerald."

Daisy scrambled the rest of the way up the ladder. She hadn't brought a flashlight, but when she was high enough to look through the opening, she realized she wasn't going to need one. The rising sun sent its rays deep into the cave. The rock pile where the bicycle lay buried was clearly visible, and there was another mound against the back wall, ten or twelve feet away.

"What can you see?" Marna asked excitedly. "Besides the bike, I mean."

"Tell you in a minute." Daisy stepped over the last

116

rung into the cave. She had to crouch to get through the opening, but the roof inside was a little higher. She dropped to her knees in front of the nearest rock pile and began brushing away dirt and some of the smaller rocks.

"What are you doing?" Marna called after a few moments. "I can't see you."

"I'm uncovering more of the bicycle," Daisy told her in a low voice. "I can see both handlebars now—it looks really old-fashioned." She crawled back to the mouth of the cave. "Are you okay?"

"Of course I'm okay," Marna retorted. "It's just boring down here, that's all." She sounded less enthusiastic now, and her voice had taken on a familiar whine. "Maybe I'll come up and watch, but I won't come in!"

"No, stay there! I'll be out in a minute." Daisy backed away from the opening. She could stand up if she kept her knees bent, but it was easier to crawl. She made her way to the back of the cave.

The second rock pile was longer than the one that covered the bicycle. Kneeling in front of it, Daisy felt a little dizzy. She began moving rocks away from one end. Her stomach churned, and she wondered if she was going to be sick.

"What's under there?"

Daisy whirled around. Marna had climbed to the top of the ladder and was squinting into the cave.

"I don't know! Go back down. Please!"

Marna stepped into the cave, almost knocking over the ladder in the process. "It's nasty in here," she complained. She glanced over at the partly uncovered bicycle and then back at the long rock pile in front of

Daisy. "Are you going to move all of that? It'll take forever."

"No, I'm not," Daisy said through gritted teeth. "Go back outside and look around, okay?"

"Why do you keep saying that?" Marna didn't move. "You know what? . . . It's scary in here, but it's scary out there, too." She seemed puzzled as she said it. "I don't know why, it just is."

Daisy's heart sank. If Marna was feeling the phantom's presence, they were running out of time. She worked faster, shoving the rocks at the top of the pile to one side so that they scattered across the floor.

"Ouch!" Marna jumped away. "That big one landed on my toe!"

"Sorry," Daisy breathed. Then she, too, rocked back on her heels. The cascading rocks had caused the end of the pile to shift. A scrap of blue cloth appeared near the bottom.

Marna saw it and came closer. "What's that?" She tugged at the ragged edge and then jerked her hand away. "Daisy?" Her voice shot up.

"I don't know," Daisy said. Her mouth was cottony dry. With trembling hands she lifted away another rock and then another to uncover more cloth.

"Don't!" Marna grabbed her arm. "Don't look any more! Let's get out of here!"

Daisy shook her head. She brushed away a big clump of dirt. The blue cloth was denim. From it protruded a long, yellowish bone that ended in a crumbling foot.

Marna made a choking sound and scrambled toward the mouth of the cave. As Daisy turned to follow, she saw the top of the ladder swing sideways and vanish. Then the light dimmed abruptly. A giant head and shoulders loomed in the opening, cutting off the sun.

Marna screamed and leaped backward. "Wh-what is it?" she wailed.

The girls clutched each other and stared at the creature that stared silently back at them.

The head was a massive chunk of wood, the upper body a tangle of driftwood, branches, and twigs. Long strands of green and brown weed hung like hair from the head and covered what might have been a face.

"It's a ghost!" Daisy said hoarsely. "It's what I saw that day at the pond."

"No, it isn't!" Marna cried. "You can't *see* a ghost! What *is* it?"

The phantom lurched backward, and once again sunlight poured into the cave. Daisy started to get up and gave a little shriek of horror as her fingers brushed the bone she'd just uncovered. Then the cave darkened again as the phantom returned. This time its arm—a long, jagged piece of driftwood—came thrusting into the cave. It swept blindly from side to side, raking Daisy's hair with splintery fingers and hovering over Marna's shoulder.

"Get back!" Daisy gasped. "Hurry!" But Marna seemed unable to move. She let Daisy drag her up onto the rock pile, and they huddled there together.

"It's going to kill us!" Marna whimpered. "What'll we do?" Both girls ducked as the arm swept toward the sound of Marna's voice.

And then, unbelievably, the giant figure exploded

with startling force. There was a crash outside, followed by a groan. Too terrified to move, the girls crouched on the rocks and stared.

"I'm going to look," Daisy whispered finally, when the mouth of the cave remained empty.

"No, it'll come back," Marna cried. "It'll hurt you!" She grabbed Daisy's arm and tried to stop her.

Daisy freed herself and crawled slowly toward the light, ready to leap to one side if the phantom reappeared. When she neared the opening, she lay flat to peer over the edge.

What she saw was astonishing. Beyond the rocks at the foot of the cliff, dozens of pieces of driftwood and branches were scattered over the sand. In their midst, lying on his back and staring up at Daisy with a look of total disbelief, was Gerald. His arms were locked tightly around two long, sturdy tree limbs.

Chapter Twenty

"Are you okay?" *Dumb question!* Daisy thought. Gerald certainly didn't look okay. His eyes were glazed, as if he were in a trance. After a moment he rolled over on his side and released his hold on the tree limbs he'd been clutching. Then he struggled to his knees and looked around at the driftwood and broken branches that littered the beach.

"Where is it?" Marna sobbed from the back of the cave. "Is it gone?"

"Come and look." Daisy made room for her at the opening. "It's not gone, exactly. It's scattered! Gerald tackled it!"

"He *tackled* it?" Marna gasped. She peeked out fearfully. "He wouldn't! That's crazy!"

Gerald stood up. "It certainly is," he agreed shakily. "I'm not the kind of person who tackles things. Especially not a *thing* like that!" He dusted off his knees and fingered the torn sleeve of his T-shirt. Then he lifted one end of the ladder that lay along the foot of the cliff and hoisted it toward the mouth of the cave.

"Come down here," he ordered. "Tell me what's going on—if that's possible!"

"You'd better come up here first," Daisy told him. "We have to show you something."

Gerald looked as if he wanted to refuse, but he changed his mind when Marna gave a startled shriek. She'd just remembered what lay behind them in the cave.

"Okay, okay," he said. "I'm coming. But if it's another whatchamacallit . . ." He climbed cautiously, until his smudged face was even with theirs.

"It's a body!" Marna squealed. "There's a body in here!"

Gerald glanced at Daisy. When she nodded, he stepped through the opening and crawled back to where she pointed. Then he sat down heavily, as if the breath had been knocked out of him by the sight of the bony foot protruding from the rock pile.

"I think I know who it is," Daisy said timidly. "There was a man who wanted to interview Morgan Trier for a book he was writing, and Thomas was worried about it. He was afraid of what Morgan might do, so he sent the guy away. But the writer came back when Thomas wasn't home, and Morgan said, 'I sent the rascal packing.' That *could* mean he killed the man and hid him and his bike in here and then closed up the cave with rocks and mortar."

"What are you talking about?" Marna demanded. "How do you know all that?"

"It's in your grandfather's diary," Daisy told her. "The part about the visitor was the last thing he wrote. I think maybe he guessed what happened. Maybe he saw the sealed-up cave and remembered that Morgan had been using mortar on the brick walk."

"But he could have looked!" Marna exclaimed. "All he had to do was open up the cave—"

"He probably didn't want to know." Gerald had been staring at the pile of stones while Daisy talked, but now he turned his back on it. "Your grandfather stayed at Five Chimneys as long as his brother lived, but after that he moved as far away as he could get. This could explain why. He probably spent the rest of his life wondering if there really had been a murder and if he could have prevented it by putting Morgan in an institution. We'll have to show the diary to the police."

Daisy felt a wave of relief wash over her. Gerald wasn't going to accuse her of making up a story this time. He had to listen, now that he'd seen the phantom of Five Chimneys himself.

"I want to get down!" Marna exclaimed. She leaned out of the cave and looked up and down the beach. "That—that thing might come back!"

Gerald crawled over and helped her out to the ladder. "Not likely," he said patiently. "He's in a hundred pieces at least. Daisy thinks it was Morgan's ghost, trying to scare us away from this place. And she's probably right. She's been right before." He smiled at Daisy apologetically. "Come on. We'll all feel better when we get some fresh air."

Daisy's knees were still trembling as she climbed

down the ladder, but she felt better with every step. She was free. Someone else could worry about Morgan Trier now.

Gerald put out a hand to stop Marna as she started toward the house. "We have to talk," he said. "This whole thing seems like a nightmare, but it did happen." He looked again at the fragments of wood. "Marna, if we tell your mother everything, she'll want to leave Five Chimneys forever."

"Good!" Marna said. "That's what I want, too."

"Are you sure?" he asked gently. "This property has belonged to your mother's family for generations. Now it belongs to her—and to you. Do you really want to let the spirit of a mentally ill man drive you away from it? If we can keep our nerve, we don't have to run away."

Marna scowled. "You're the only one who likes it here," she grumbled.

Gerald shook his head. "That's not true. I love it, but your mother loves it, too. And it's a wonderful place for Patty to grow up in. Who knows, you might even get to like it yourself some day."

"But it's dangerous," Marna argued. "That . . . Uncle Morgan's spirit could still be around. Even if you stopped him this time, he could come back!"

"Maybe," Gerald admitted. "But maybe not. Thanks to Daisy, we've already discovered something very ugly that he wanted to hide. If I'd listened to her when she tried to tell me what she suspected about Morgan—how he might be the one causing our problems—he might not have had a chance to scare all three of us half to death this morning. Anyway, from now on we'll know who the enemy is." He paused. "I think we could handle it together, don't you?"

Something flickered in Marna's eyes. *She knows he saved our lives*, Daisy thought. *She wants to go on hating him, but she can't.*

"How about it?" Gerald persisted. "Daisy's been doing our worrying for us up to now. Do you think you and I can take over?"

Reluctantly, Marna nodded. "I guess."

"Good!" Gerald was beginning to sound more like himself. "Then the first thing we're going to do is gather up all the pieces of wood lying around here and burn them." He grinned at the girls' horrified expressions. "If we leave this mess where it is, the police are going to wonder about it when they come to check out what's in the cave. We can tell them we've been cleaning up the beach, and that'll be the truth."

They set to work. Later, while the bonfire blazed, they discussed how much of their adventure they could safely tell. . . .

The girls had wanted to search the cave before it was sealed. . . .

Gerald had come down to the beach and had heard them screaming. . . .

At first he hadn't believed they'd actually found a body, but then he'd climbed up to look for himself. . . .

"And that's all," Gerald said. "The phantom has to be our secret—for now, at least—just the three of us. Trish will be upset enough when she hears about the body, and it'll be hard on Patty, too."

Daisy stared at the blazing chunk of wood that had

been the phantom's head. "I'm going to tell my mom," she said. "She won't tell anyone if I ask her not to. She'll just listen."

"The way I should have listened," Gerald said. "I think you and your mother must be a lot alike, Daisy. You certainly don't give up when you want to find out what's going on. Maybe someday you'll be a journalist, too. Your editor will ask you to write about the strangest experience you've ever had, and you'll think of your visit here."

"You can come back next summer, if you want," Marna said in an offhand way, as if it didn't matter much, either way. "Maybe—maybe you and your mother could come to one of our Mystery Weekends."

Our Mystery Weekends. Daisy saw Gerald's look; he was pleasantly surprised. And she knew right then that, even though she was counting the hours till her mother came for her, she wanted to see the Graveses again. All of them.

"I'd like to come back," she said, and she smiled at Marna until, finally, Marna had to smile, too. "Our families would have fun together."

Epilogue

He stood near the road, beside the little stone building where his parents and grandparents had stored their vegetables. From the direction of the house came the sound of voices calling good-bye. The small blind child's cries rose above the rest.

When the car bumped past him, he glared at the girl who was smiling happily at the woman driving. He hated that nosy girl. If she hadn't come to Five Chimneys and discovered his secret, he might have convinced the others that they didn't want to stay here. By this time he might have had his kingdom to himself—forever.

He started back toward the house. It had been his castle once, and now that the girl was gone, he could try to claim it again. But he was very tired, and the people in the house were growing stronger. They now knew who he was—and they'd be ready for him.

Perhaps he would let them think they had won. The kingdom would still belong to him at night, when they were sleeping, and when storms drove them inside, away from his beach.